the krracts encounter

Dave and Kim,
I present this book to my great friends and neighbors. I hope you enjoy it.
The Zen Master,
Bob

robert woodard

Copyright © 2009 Robert Woodard
All rights reserved.
ISBN: 1-4392-5100-2
ISBN-13: 9781439251003
Visit www.booksurge.com to order additional copies.

To Gert for keeping me focused on completing what I started.

krracts pronunciations

Titles:
Krracts…………..Cracks
Byf………………Biff
Sli………………..Slee

Character Names:
Synska…………...Sin-ska
Brk'erst………….Breck-urst
V'sdntil………….Vee-said-nil
Lridniig………….Lee-rid-nige

Ship Names:
Bfnor Torrnt…….Biff-Nor Tore-rent
Ghonfuf…………Gee-hun-fuf
Piirfh Njyfn……..Pie-eye-riff Nee-jy-fin
Tuilmf…………..Too-ill-miff
Njyfur Lguunc….Nee-jy-fur Lee-goo-unc
Kaffnur Dneui….Kaf-newer Dee-nee-you-e

Weapon:
Keddrft Jractk….Ked-drift Jee-rack-tack

Misc:
Ghugg…………...Gee-hug
Fnifs……………..Fee-niffs

the krracts encounter
prologue

With raw materials on Earth pretty much gone, a group of investors formed Mercantile Enterprises in the year 2215. Their charter was to find lifeless planets for the mining of raw materials. This started with the company receiving mining rights on nearby moons in the Earth's solar system. Miners soon began harvesting the raw materials, providing the return on investments anticipated. As the company grew, so did its mining operation. Profits provided financing to expand mining operations outward toward more and more uninhabited planets and moons. The larger the operations became the more need for efficiency grew. Both in support of mining crews and in the transport of raw materials one way, supplies the other.

The next step in improving efficiency was to set up a mining operation on the planet surface. In the company's early days, miners lived aboard a supply ship and were shuttled to the surface each day. Work was slow and hazardous. Should a worker puncture an environmental suit, it was almost sure death. It was determined that these miners needed a safer way to work in these inhospitable environments. Older spacecraft were purchased for refitting, and then sent out with trained crews to set up environmental stations. A mining crew was sent down to the newly built stations to harvest what resources they could. Starting with a single setup ship, transport, and two mining crews the company had grown to five setup ships, eleven transports, and seventeen mining crews.

Company probes soon began traveling through space in search of new planets or moons to harvest. Planets and moons that showed a good promise for mining were cataloged. Along with finding lifeless planets, the probes often came back with data on planets that had potential for sustaining life. That data was sold to the governments back on Earth for future exploration. Over time, some of these planets were set up with outposts that became colonies. Mercantile Enterprises often took advantage of these new colonies by leasing docking berths and living quarters from the space ports that sprang up to handle shipping. The company held leasing rights with several colonies in space. These became home to setup ships and mining crews, allowing the distance to be shortened to and from newly discovered planets or moons. Mercantile Enterprises was now the third largest company by net worth and supplied nearly eighty percent of all natural resources used back on Earth.

Three orbiting stations revolved around the colonized planet Rapitine. They were labeled Rap-1, Rap-2 and Rap-3. Rap-1 handled all incoming and outgoing shipping. Rap-2 housed a military fleet that kept the peace among colonies. Most of this military fleet was left over from an earlier campaign to rid the shipping lanes from well-organized raiders. This military presence helped to discourage any future would-be merchant raiders, along with keeping peace among the various shipping companies. Rap-3 was an overflow station, now home to two of Mercantile Enterprise's setup ships, three transports, and five mining crews. One of the two setup ships was the Privateer.

The Privateer had been purchased just after the end of the raider campaign in 2238. Originally built as an escort class destroyer, her main duty was part of a convoy escort team. She had escorted merchant ships through the shipping lanes to provide supplies and trade goods across the various colonies. The Privateer's career was filled with early battles with raiders attempting to team up on the convoys. She wore many battle scars before a hunter-seeker fleet was established to take the fight to the raiders themselves. It took only fourteen months with seek and destroy tactics to break the backs of the raiders and eliminate piracy. The majority of this hunter-seeker fleet was now stationed at Rap-2.

No longer needed, the Privateer was rescued from mothballing to be refitted for her new duties. The large, multiple storage bays originally used to carry and service her missiles and rockets were replaced with a single storage bay for handling building materials. The machine shop was expanded to handle the needs of both ship repairs and building setup. Stamping machines were added to mold thick plastic sheets into the shapes needed to construct a building. Over time, the crews learned that the easiest way to work through a setup was to build the supply warehouse first, then transfer the machinery to complete the remaining buildings. This offered more room to work while also allowing unformed sheets to be placed into the shuttles in large quantities rather than loading them in after they'd become oddly shaped panels.

The Privateer kept her top turret mount containing a twin-barreled gun. Originally, the gun and supporting compartments were to be replaced to expand storage capacity; however, the Privateer contained absorption-based shielding, which would have required it to be upgraded to deflection-based shielding. It was determined that keeping the gun was cheaper and allowed the Privateer to be operational two months earlier than originally planned.

The Privateer was in service for just over two years when a transport exploded after colliding with a small meteor upon exiting warp. Maritime law required all vessels to be upgraded to deflection-based shielding, which was designed to repel objects from the hull rather than absorbing them. While the Privateer was being refitted with the shielding, another vote was taken at removing the gun emplacement. It was decided that more money would be lost in the cost of removal, restructuring of the workspaces, and time lost, as opposed to just keeping a small gun crew on staff, so the gun emplacement had stubbornly stayed with the ship.

Unlike the other setup ships, the Privateer was the only vessel retrofitted from a military design. The other setup ships having been converted from commercial freighters. She was faster and more maneuverable than the other setup ships. Her one major drawback was having less storage capacity than regular freighters. This limited her ability; she could only setup one planet per trip. The Privateer was the last of the converted ships. The company's focus shifted to purchasing newer ships, which were designed and built for the sole purpose of setting up planets for habitation. One by one, the older ships were being replaced with newer, more efficient vessels. The Privateer, being the last ship converted, would be last to be replaced. The company was on a pace to replace one ship every fifteen months. There were also plans to expand the setup fleet to eight ships.

The downside of being assigned to the Privateer was that the company usually gave them the most time-consuming assignments. Since maritime law restricted how long a crew could be kept in space travel, the company gave the Privateer assignments that had the longest expected setup time. This allowed the larger setup ships to focus on quicker setups where two or more could be done in the time it would take the Privateer's crew to do one.

The crew of the Privateer had just completed construction on the last of the environmental buildings. The year was 2246. But something was happening in another system not too far away...

Chapter One

Probe 13-115-98 was on the outbound leg of its journey. It dropped into another system to begin mapping all the planets, moons and satellites located within it's scanning range. Once completed, it selected the closest planet and began a more detailed mapping. Using various scanning methods it measured planet density, core deposit potential and overall planet composite.

Completed, the probe made an exit vector for departing the system. About halfway there it detected a large object coming into its path. The probe deviated around the large object and continued on its way. It detected smaller objects coming up from behind but ignored them as they passed by. Oblivious to any trouble, the probe ran smack into its own destruction.

"Damn it Sharon! Another week?" Linda yelled.

"That's what they said, Captain," Sharon responded.

"What's their excuse this time?" Linda asked.

"It's still the wind. While it dropped down to sixty knots, it is still too high for them to work outside and get them in place," Sharon answered.

"You get back down there and tell that chief engineer that he has two days to get it done. On the third day, I am weighing anchor and the Privateer is sailing for home, with or without them aboard," Linda ordered. She was tired of all the delays she had been dealing with so far. She picked up a piece of paper from her desk and waved it at Sharon saying, "You know what this is? It's another damn message from the execs at Mercantile Enterprises; they have been chewing on my butt these last few weeks, because of these delays. They keep reminding me that they have reserved a slot with the shipyards for our overhaul. If we miss it, we get to spend another couple months station side, waiting for another berth to open up."

"Unless the wind cooperates there really isn't much they can do, Captain," Sharon argued.

"They can still make up the rest of the walls and get them all ready to install. If we have to leave them in the warehouse, the miners can complete the installation when they arrive, can they not?" Linda questioned.

"Probably, but you know they will raise holy hell with the company. They will complain that it's not in there contract to set them up," Sharon reminded Linda.

"Perhaps, but by then we will be safely out of sight again on another job. So who cares if they complain?" Linda noted. After a brief pause she added, "The Privateer leaves in three days. As the executive officer you better have this ship ready to leave."

Linda returned to her work, a clear message to Sharon that the conversation was over. Sharon turned and left the captain's cabin. She had no desire to return to the planet surface and argue it out with that stubborn chief engineer. But she also knew that if the Privateer wasn't ready to go in three days, she may be left on the planet surface herself. Linda was not the kind of captain to be ignored.

"I wonder where Bill is right now," Sharon thought out loud. She figured that if someone needed to go down and have it out with them pigheaded engineers, it would be good experience for him. She headed off to find him.

❖ ❖ ❖

Overlord jeftrk byf stood looking out the entrance to his ghugg. Dug deep into the hillside, his cave-like dwelling held a large harem. He glanced down on the nearby dwellings that were home to the many functions of the Council. It had only been about a thousand solar cycles since the krracts had formed into a society where krracts males could live this close together. Krracts were hunters by nature and fierce in their protection of mature females. In the past, this many males together would have produced many deadly fights. Even today, fights could break out, usually among overlords. Jeftrk byf considered himself beyond such nonsense. But he was a fully mature male harboring a large harem already. He could afford to lose a few females without much disruption within the ghugg.

Looking into the sun, he could feel the heat another day would bring. By mid-day, he expected the temperature to reach a comfortable one hundred thirty degrees. Behind him in the ghugg, he could hear the lings playing. The overlord tried to remember being a ling, but with his long life cycle, he couldn't. He didn't remember anything about being an underling, or overling for that matter. He did remember a lot of his underlord duties. But mostly, he remembered his accomplishments as an overlord, that led to his eventual receipt of the byf title. He was hoping to begin testing soon for that elusive sli title. With that, there was a possibility of his being selected as a member of the Council. Being a Council member was the highest honor a krracts could achieve.

Jeftrk byf stepped onto the walkway leading down the hillside, toward the Council complexes. The building his working area resided in was used strictly to support space activity. His area was dedicated strictly to the support of the small fleet of minelayers that roamed in and around the krracts system. So repetitious was his walk that he hardly even noticed his surroundings anymore.

Finally reaching the building, the overlord entered. He dreaded walking past the empty spaces that once housed the workers of the once mighty fleet. All those warships were now permanently docked overhead at the direction of the Council.

Thinking back to the days when he worked aboard and finally commanded a warship. Those were the glory days when the Council laid claim to all of krracts space. Only the addition of light speed, capable drives kept the fleet active when the excitement began to fizzle. These new drives allowed war ships to quickly reach a nearby planet and examine it for life. It was also hoped that some new species would be discovered that would add new hunting prospects for the krracts males. But when none came to fruition, the allure wore off among the overlords. The Council could see that underlords would lose interest in becoming overlords if it required being aboard a war ship. One by one, these ships were assigned to a docking berth where they were dying a slow death. Crews were reassigned to other duties. Today, only a skeleton crew existed to insure each ship was kept in readiness in case they were ever needed again. All of the overlords, those still living, had moved on to other positions within the Council support structure, including jeftrk byf.

Entering his working space, jeftrk byf walked over to the large wall chart to review the current location of each minelayer. He could see that he had two docked. One being resupplied while the other was receiving minor repairs. He currently had three others on assignment. He paused as he looked at the brown-colored pin that represented the ship bfnor torrnt. They were right on schedule, which was good considering that this ship was under the direction of a new overlord. He had recommended this overlord's testing for a byf title a while back. He also knew this overlord was well-qualified to command a ship. This overlord, synska byf, had served as his underlord in the past. He had performed his duty well enough.

Sighing, jeftrk byf walked over to his desk and sat behind it. There were already daily reports waiting for his review before they were passed on to the Council members. The overling had placed these in order of importance based on his opinion of each subject matter. He picked up the first sheet. It was a clearance order for one of the minelayers. Another sheet was attached that outlined the work assignment the ship would resume once it left the docking facility. He stamped the release order and work assignment with his seal. Moving this to the routing box, he moved on to the next sheet. It was an updated work assessment on the ship being repaired. More structural fatigue was found in the aft launch bay. "More delays," he mumbled as he made an entry in his to-do log to extend the work assignments of the other ships.

The overling walking into his office made jeftrk byf look up from the latest report he was reviewing. The overling was updating the wall chart to reflect the latest communiqués. The overlord had completed the last of the daily reports at about the same time that the overling had completed the updates to the chart. The overling quickly grabbed the signed reports and headed off to deliver them before the Council met that morning. Jeftrk byf decided to refresh his mind before he jumped into his to-do list. He looked out the window and watched some underlings as they cleaned the area around the building across the walkway. He watched with interest as an overling directed the work. He again tried to recall his days as an overling. It was just too long ago, he thought. He wondered if he would ever get onto the Council. He knew that he was so close to getting his sli title. He had even made a few recommendations for improvement to the Council members that were eventually adopted. The byf title was earned through strength testing, but the sli title was granted only to those that showed high levels of intelligence.

He remembered the last recommendation he'd made; it was just now being looked into. He had become aware of an accidental discovery by an overling working in the research group. The overling had been trying to improve the routing efficiency of electrical current or some such nonsense (jeftrk byf was not much for science) when he made the discovery that electrical current could be generated by the sun. It was never determined what purpose this could serve until jeftrk byf suggested the possibility of mines and buoys being powered this way. Reducing the fuel consumption with this discovery could increase the time a buoy or mine ran without needing servicing. He had also recommended launching mines and buoys from the planet's surface, thereby reducing the servicing needs of each of the minelayers. That one was shot down by the Council as unpractical. "Well, at least they know who I am now," he said out loud.

Walking over to the wall chart again, he reviewed the updates. He wished he was on one of the ships again. He wondered where that thought came from. He always felt confined on a ship and could not wait to return. Was it the freedom of being away from the continuous demands of the Council? He shook off his thoughts and concentrated on the chart again. He could see that the bfnor torrnt was nearing the end of its assignment. He wondered if it was wise to increase their workload, being his first assignment and all. But he didn't feel he had much choice with the other minelayer in repairs longer than anticipated. After a few beats, he returned to his desk and began to review his to-do list. This was going to be another long day.

❖ ❖ ❖

Overlord synska byf was sitting on the bridge of the bfnor torrnt, Tail Whip, while overlings and underlings were getting ready to push a tracking buoy out the right side loading bay. Underlord brk'erst was overseeing the work, so the overlord knew that it would be done correctly. This was synska byf's first command of a ship and only two solar cycles after becoming a byf. He was sure that overlord jeftrk byf had played a role in his recommendation for this command. With his former overlord working directly for the Council, that recommendation would have carried a lot of weight. The prior overlord of the bfnor torrnt was killed in a fight with another overlord in a dispute over a den bound female. This timely death gave synska byf the opportunity he needed to assume command of this ship.

The overlord was busy watching the work being performed via the monitor by his command chair. It was dangerous work because someone could make the mistake of opening the inner hatch while the outer hatch was still open. Built as a minelayer, his ship was also used to carry and deploy these buoys wherever the Counsel deemed necessary. They kept him busy by having him run all over the galaxy to lay and retrieve mines, and set and service buoys. With the rest of the once mighty fleet sitting in space docks, he seldom ran across other ships. It was always a real pleasure when they had to come in for supplies or to make repairs.

An overling handled the controls that worked the mechanical arms mounted between the inner and outer hatches. The jaw-like clamps at the end of each arm grabbed the sidebars of the buoy. Slowly, the buoy lifted off the deck as the magnetic locks released their grip. Once clear of the deck, the mechanical arms turned the buoy towards the open outer hatch and released their grip. The buoy slowly drifted out the opening and away from the ship. The outer hatch was closed and the clean-up process began.

Pushing the monitor away, the overlord stood up to begin pacing about the bridge. He was always antsy whenever his ship was sitting in one place for too long. It had already been a long day, and he wanted the underlord to take command of the bridge so he could head for his living space located one deck below and almost directly under the bridge. Stopping back at his command chair, he looked at his monitor and could see the underlings cleaning up the area. Any overling could take over this part of the supervision, so the underlord should be on his way back to the bridge. He continued his pacing while glancing at the communication overling during each pass. The overling was establishing a communication link with the drifting buoy. He looked at the main monitor that now showed the buoy as it continued to drift away from the side of his ship.

Returning to the bridge, brk'erst informed synska byf of the buoy's status. When he completed his report, he walked over to the communication station and asked, "Overling, is the communication link with the buoy established yet?"

"Yes, Underlord. The buoy has completed the extension of its positional antenna. I have a link between the ship's computer and the buoy's guidance system. The buoy is now ready to have the rotational and positional commands fed in," he replied.

Brk'erst gave the overling the okay to feed in the needed command entries. With the commands fed in the buoy moved to its assigned location. A confirmation message confirmed the buoy had completed its positioning.

With the buoy set, the communications overling returned to his regular duty of monitoring transmission frequencies. This was the most boring part of his assignment. Messages to and from the ship usually came in spurts with long delays in between. He settled into his stool to begin the routine of rotating through the multitude of frequencies they monitored.

Using the pointed claws of his hands, the overling slid the various controls back and forth to reduce the background noises of space. He listened to the white noise of space hiss in his ear-set. His sensitive hearing was able to detect a faint signal out of the other noises. He slowly reversed the disc in an attempt to strengthen the signal. Adjusting other controls helped him pull in the weak signal. He started recording the transmission until he was sure that he had captured a full cycle of the recurring message. He then fed the recording through a translator and waited for the results. The overling knew that the signal was from one of their own buoys. The computer did not take long to confirm this.

Getting ready to leave the bridge, synska byf was giving brk'erst final orders for getting the ship underway. Synska byf had turned to leave the bridge while brk'erst heading for the command chair. Synska byf stopped when he heard the overling speak.

"Overlord, I am picking up a transmission from a tracking buoy. I have recorded the message for playback," relayed the overling.

"Have it transferred to my command console immediately, overling," the overlord responded as he headed back to his chair. His feet pounded loudly on the decking from his three hundred plus weight.

Brk'erst moved out of the way, allowing the overlord to take command again. Once seated, synska byf waited for the communication file to transfer to his console. Once completed, the overlord played the message that contained both text and digital readout. The overlord tapped on one of his long sharp fangs with a claw, as he observed the message. The length of the four fangs that protruded from the upper and lower jaws helped determine the maturity of the male krracts. The fangs grew longer as the krracts male aged.

The message relayed the buoy's observation of a small metal object that dropped out of light speed as it entered the rhepp system. A two-dimensional image was shown of the object. The message noted the course and speed of the object as it was recorded by the buoy. Synska byf could see that it was a small object about half the size of the buoy; however, he did not recognize the characteristics of it.

Synska byf moved the console so brk'erst could see the message as he replayed it. When the replay ended, brk'erst said, "The overling told me that the signal is so weak that he doubted it made it to the Council. The buoy must have a weak transmitter. The Council will be very interested in seeing this message. Do you want me to hold off on getting the ship underway while you communicate with them, Overlord?"

"No. Proceed as planned while I send a message to the Council. I intend to request permission to investigate this strange object. There is always a chance that the Council will send another ship or just opt to observe what the buoy captures. Seeing how we are closest to this system, we may get a chance to investigate it. I will be in my living space," synska byf answered while he transferred the message to the communication station in his living space. He then stood up and headed off the bridge.

Once in his living space, synska byf had sent a message to the Council with the buoy's message attached. He had paced about the small area until a reply had been received. He was ordered to break off from his current assignment, investigate the object, and retrieve tracking data from the buoy itself. He was also instructed to attempt to capture the object so the Council could study it. With his orders and the location of the buoy in hand, he headed for the bridge.

THE KRRACTS ENCOUNTER 11

"Underlord, prepare to alter course," synska byf said as he walked onto the bridge. He continued, "I have the jump vector here." He handed brk'erst the sheet he had written it on before continuing, "Make preparations for jumping to light speed. We will enter the rhepp system at the vector point noted. Alter course as soon as the navigational entries have been calculated."

With the new course entered, the bfnor torrnt headed for the jump point. Upon reaching it, they made the jump to light speed. Thirty-seven beat cycles later, the bfnor torrnt dropped out of light speed.

"Perform a quick scan of the area. Let me know what is picked up. Begin braking," ordered synska byf.

The scanning overling began a quick sweep of the system. "I have the tracking buoy on station. I am also picking up an unknown object on an intersecting course to our current track. All other sectors are clear. I am placing the tracking display on the view screen," he reported.

The large view screen, located at the front of the bridge, was showing a forward view from the ship. A square section, which took up a quarter of the viewing space, blacked out. It was shortly filled with a tracking image showing the object. Below the image of the object, a sensor reading was being displayed.

Looking at the new image, brk'erst commented, "The object appears to be heading out of the system. It has detected us and is now altering course to pass by. Sensor readings are showing a minimal deviation pattern."

Brk'erst began reading off the sensor information for the overlord. "Object is metallic in design. Type of composite is unknown. Energy output is high, but energy signature is unknown. Ionization output is normal. No signal output is being detected. The ship's computer does not show any known classification for this object. We have come across something never before recorded."

Walking closer to the view screen, brk'erst continued, "Very strange design. It seems to be aware of our presence, but it is only veering slightly to avoid us. Object speed is three hundred fifty ten-fnifs and ninety-nine per beat."

Synska byf watched the object until it was just about even with his ship. He then commented, "Whatever the purpose is for this object, the Council wants us to capture it so they can look it over. Overling, fire a shot in front of the object to see if we can get it to stop. Be ready to fire another round into the object should it continue on course. Set power output to half strength. I don't want to fry its electronic components."

Brk'erst relayed the order to the overling at the weapons console. The overling fired the main cannons so the beam would pass directly in front of the object's path. The energy beam could be seen in the viewer as it crossed in front of the object, but it had no visible effect.

Brk'erst relayed to his overlord, "Tracking shows no change in energy output readings. The object is still on course with no detectable variance in heading. Weapon's tracking has locked on the target. Power setting at half strength. Ready to fire on your orders."

"Fire," ordered synska byf.

Once again, brk'erst relayed the command. The overling fired a short burst at the fleeing object. The energy beam seemed to bend slightly as it neared the target to pass above it. Synska byf looked back at brk'erst, who was validating that the target was locked on. Brk'erst said, "Target lock is confirmed. I show no angle variation factored into the shot."

Synska byf was concerned about the distance the object was putting between itself and his ship. The object had completed its deviation around his ship and was speeding away. With the speed of his ship, still in braking mode, and the speed of the object itself, it would not be long before the two were out of range. He ordered, "Increase energy output to full and fire again."

The overling adjusted the power output while waiting for a target lock validation. To increase the chance of a hit, brk'erst had the overling widen the energy beam. This would reduce the hit's effect, but it would create a wider band to the target. Satisfied with the results, he told the overling to fire.

The beam shot straight at the target, but then appeared to split as it passed over the top and under the bottom of the object. They both looked at each other. There was no doubt between them that the shot was on target. They both saw that the beam had been split to pass by harmlessly.

Brk'erst could tell that synska byf was beginning to lose his patience with this object. The overlord asked sharply, "Underlord, what kind of mines are loaded in the aft tubes?"

Checking the status board, brk'erst answered, "I show all four tubes contain proximity mines."

Synska byf swore softly before saying, "I would have preferred linked mines, but we will have to make the proximity's work. Select all four mines into the weapon's tracking computer. Have them launched to pass by the object on all sides. Allow enough room for the mines to arm before the object catches up again. If it passes by one of the mines at the same distance it passed by us, it should detonate it. Set the detection field to maximum. We will only get one shot at this, so make it good, underlord."

Brk'erst watched over the overling as he quickly entered the information into the computer. Having directed the computer to fire the rear tubes in order, the overling pressed the fire button. The deck vibrated with the release of each mine. The overhead lighting dimmed to match the vibration as the massive coils struggled to handle the added energy needs each tube took to propel a mine. Each mine came into view on the tracking display as they raced away from the ship. Flashes could be seen as the propulsion on each of them fired off.

The object was now too far away to see clearly. Brk'erst watched on the display screen as each mine passed by the object. Each mine shut down its propulsion and began braking. As each mine began to slow, its magnetic field activated to full range. All four mines were now armed and ready to explode on anything that broke the magnetic field. The four mines, taking up position, covered a square patterned area ahead of the object. The detection field of each mine barely overlapped in the middle of the square.

The object continued on its course. Brk'erst expected it to veer away at any moment to avoid the mines. When it did not deviate from its course, brk'erst knew that it could not get around any of the four mines without hitting a magnetic field. It soon became apparent that the object was not going to alter course at all. He looked away as the four mines exploded in unison.

The screen still registered the brightness from the multiple explosions as synska byf looked back at the image. The tracking computer was being overloaded by the results of the blasts. As the effects of the blast slowly died away, the sensor readings returned to normal. The area around the blast was still covered in a cloud of burning particles. The tracking computer was no longer showing any signs of the object. It was gone, apparently blasted into a million tiny, burning particles that would leave nothing to tell its tale.

Synska byf stood up from his command chair. He motioned brk'erst over to him. Once together, the overlord said, "My instructions were to return the object to the Council for study. Even though we did not allow the object to leave this area, the Council members will not be pleased with its destruction. I will be leaving to communicate my findings. Once braking is complete, alter course to come alongside the buoy. I want all tracking data contained within the buoy transferred to the ship's computer. Have an overling strip off all data related to this object. Once this is complete, have the overling begin reviewing the tracking data from both the ship and buoy to determine what the object was doing here."

Back in his living space, synska byf paced back and forth. He was trying to formulate the message he would send back to the Council. Having all the aft tubes loaded with only proximity mines had come back to haunt him. Just one linked mine would have prevented this catastrophe. He could have controlled the ignition point of a linked mine. Had he acted sooner he possibly could have turned the ship so it was pointed at the object, where the linked mines were already loaded in the front tubes. But the speed of the object and his ship made everything happen so quickly. Could I have done something different, he wondered? He stopped his pacing to think this over. Shaking his head he paced about again. Well, how was he going to explain all this without sounding incompetent, he wondered? He figured he had stalled long enough; he sat down to write out his report for sending to the Council. Perhaps his final report, he fretted.

chapter two

Lieutenant Rebecca Ladd swung the shuttle around as a dust-off prior to attempting to land. The dry, loose soil swirled around, making visibility near zero out her cockpit. The sixty-five-mile-an-hour wind was not helping matters either. She concentrated on her strut indicators that were showing distance-to-ground clearance for both front and back sections of each skid. It was tricky trying to keep her shuttle level in such violent wind. She cringed when the shuttle bounced off the tip of one skid before settling to the ground. She quickly shut the turbines and thrusters down.

Rebecca waited for a ground worker to get a sled under her shuttle so it could be pulled into the storage building. She didn't have to wait long before she felt the shuttle being elevated off the ground. She wondered how they could have seen well enough to guide the sled under her shuttle without hitting anything. She was still unable to see clearly through the swirling dust outside her cockpit windshield. Her shuttle shook slightly as she felt the pull of the sled. A few minutes later, the shuttle was inside the protective walls of the storage building behind large double doors. She felt the shuttle being lowered back down on its landing skids.

Squirming out of the cockpit seat, she headed back towards the storage section of the shuttle. She opened the side access door. Before stepping out, she grabbed a breathing mask and slipped the adjustable strap over her head so the mask hung on her chest. She didn't need the mask in the building, but everyone was required to carry one in case of an emergency. She could smell the musty odor caused by the environmental units. Stepping out onto the thin metal sheeting that made up the floor, she walked to the back of the shuttle. She activated the rear cargo hatch release. The whine of the hydraulic units signaled the opening of the rear hatch as it was raised. The lower end of the hatch lid just cleared the ceiling as it reached its fully open position. She stepped aside as an engineer guided the small forklift into place to lift the first bundle of plastic sheeting out of the hold. To each side of the stack were long metal poles that ran the full length of the shuttle's cargo space. She knew these would have to be unloaded by hand.

Looking around at the multitude of activities underway around her, Rebecca waited for the workers to unload her shuttle. In one area, machines were being used to soften and shape plastic sheeting. This always fascinated her. In another area, a group of engineers put these plastic shapes together with odd-shaped fasteners. A couple officers were standing in a corner trying to hold a conversation in the noisy building. She recognized one as Commander Launtra, but the other had her back to her, so she wasn't able to tell who it was. She shrugged her shoulders and retreated into the cockpit to wait for her return trip. With the work here just about done, she would be hauling unneeded equipment back to the ship. All in a day's work, she thought to herself.

Once again in the cramped confines of her pilot's seat, she put her hands behind her head and relaxed. Music was playing from the recorder taped to the main control panel. She had listened to all of the recordings so many times that it was only noise now. With her return home nearing, she started thinking about what she would do with her few months off. She had almost dozed off when one of the engineers startled her by saying, "Load's out."

Before he could finish his statement, Rebecca yelled, "Sheesh, Eric, you scared the shit out of me. Don't be sneaking up on me like that unless you want my boot print implanted on your backside."

Eric laughed as he crawled into the co-pilot's seat next to her and noticed that she wasn't even wearing boots. She was wearing cross-strapped sandals. "Sorry, I didn't know you were so sensitive."

"Go to hell," she snapped back.

"Anyway, we will begin loading in the two extra stamping machines that aren't needed anymore. We should have you out of here in about twenty minutes." Eric was looking out the side window as he spoke. From his position, he could see one of the machines being raised by a hand-run lift. Looking back at Rebecca, he asked, "You have any plans when you get back to the station?"

"Not really. I haven't decided what I want to do yet. My contract will be up after this run, so I may look around and see what else is out there. I like this job, but it might be interesting to pick up a job ferrying people back and forth from the planet to the stations. I could stay closer to civilization, which would keep me from having to be away so much. These long setups are really screwing up my love life," she responded.

"Yea, I here ya. I have two more tours on my contract before I can start looking around again. I'm not sure what else I would want to do, though. This job isn't too bad, and the pay is good. I can usually save about half the credits I build up each time we go out. The way I figure it, if I did this for another ten years, I would have enough to retire on, especially if I stayed over at one of the outposts. You can always find something to do to earn a little extra spending credits when you need them."

The shuttle shook as the first stamping machine was lifted into the shuttle and moved forward. Rebecca looked over her shoulder to verify that they were latching it down properly. She said, "Having the opportunity to build credit is a major benefit of this job, that is for sure. But, you know it gets kind of lonely not having anyone to spend it with. There just isn't a whole lot to do at the Rap stations or the planet, for that matter. It gets pretty boring after a while. Enjoying the night life is good for a week or so, but then it gets pretty tiring." She interrupted herself to yell back, "Hey! Make sure those straps are tight this time. I don't want those bastards shifting on me while I'm fighting the wind out there. The last load you meatballs put in here shifted all over the place before I got back to the ship. The supply officer chewed my ass off when he saw it." She then looked at Eric and shrugged her shoulders before turning forward again.

Eric looked back out the window and saw the second machine being pulled towards the back of the shuttle. He said as he got up, "They are about done, so I better take a look at what's going on back there. See ya next trip. Good thing I'm not fat," he said as he squeezed through the narrow opening between the two seats.

Rebecca went back to her thoughts as she waited to get clearance to leave. It wasn't long before she heard the shuttle's rear hatch being lowered. She got up and walked back to the storage area. She double-checked the straps on each of the large machines as well as the tie-downs on the smaller items that were thrown in. She also took notice of how the items were placed in the storage area to insure that the weight was distributed evenly. Walking around the shuttle, she made sure everything was in its place. As she reached the rear section, she checked the hatch to insure it was securely in place, a common safety measure just in case something had gotten caught between the hatch and the seal. Discovering a vacuum leak after exiting the atmosphere was not a pleasant event, she mused. Another engineer met her at the side hatch. He handed her a sheet that listed what was now loaded onto the shuttle.

"Here's the returning inventory list. Oh, and Commander Launtra said to tell you that he would be returning with you. He said not to bother pulling up a jump seat because he will use the co-pilot seat. We are just about ready to push you back out again. As soon as the commander is on board, we will give you the go."

Rebecca was glad that the commander was willing to squeeze into the co-pilot's chair. Even though the seats rotated down into the floor and were easy to set back upright, she just didn't feel like messing with one of them. She took the sheet and thanked him before returning to the shuttle to wait for the commander. She busily completed the checklist as the commander slipped into the seat next to her. She said, "Hello, Commander. All set to go?"

He answered, "Yep. We can take off as soon as you are ready."

"Thank you, Commander. I am almost done with pre-flight. Be sure to buckle up," she replied. She then looked out the left portal and waved to the ground crew who was waiting for her clearance to lift the shuttle.

"You sure picked a nice day for flying," the commander commented. "You sure you can get this flying toolbox off the ground?"

"Don't insult my ship, Commander. Unless you've learned to fly it is the only way you will be getting back to the Privateer," Rebecca joked.

"My apologies, Lieutenant. I am sure this is the best shuttle in the entire fleet," Bill answered back with a smile.

With the shuttle now positioned outside and ready, Rebecca prepared for liftoff. "Hang onto your hat, Commander, here we go!" she said.

The shuttle lifted off and shot skyward. Both occupants were pushed back into their cushioned seats. As the ship came into view, she began to bleed off speed using the forward jets. She used more aggressive jet thrusts as the ship became larger in the front window.

"Nice takeoff. When you make the next trip, would you pick up my spine? I think I left it back on the surface," Commander Launtra joked.

Rebecca chuckled. She liked the commander and his causal way of keeping everyone at ease around him. She was fast approaching the ship and didn't have time to hold a conversation. She joked, "I'll have you home in a few moments now, Commander. Thank you for flying shuttle express. If you have the guts, we'll haul your butts."

The forward jets were fully activated now as Rebecca continued to reduce the shuttle's speed. Experience had taught her at what speed the shuttle handled best for entry into a shuttle bay. She flipped another switch that activated the microphone in her headset. "Privateer, this is inbound shuttle three requesting permission to board and land."

Static played back into her ear for several seconds before she received a reply. "Shuttle three, this is the Privateer. You are cleared to land in shuttle bay two, repeat, shuttle bay two. Use entry lane four, repeat, entry lane four."

After waiting a couple seconds, Rebecca acknowledged with, "Privateer, this is shuttle three. Acknowledge entry, using lane four in shuttle bay two. Expected arrival in three minutes."

"Shuttle three, Privateer. Acknowledge arrival in three minutes. Shuttle bay two doors are being opened now."

Rebecca carefully entered the shuttle bay and landed the shuttle smoothly.

"Well done, pilot. I would fly with you anytime," Commander Launtra complimented as he released his straps and rose out of the chair.

"Thank you, Commander. It was a pleasure to have you aboard," Rebecca responded to the commander's back as he walked away.

A computer-generated alarm woke Commander Bill Launtra out of his slumber. Opening his eyes, he took a few moments to organize his thoughts. Bill glanced over to see the status displays that showed clearly in the darkness of the cabin. All the status lights were green. The computer-controlled cabin lights provided a dim glow, enough for Bill to see his surroundings while allowing his eyes to adjust from the darkness. Bill threw off the single light cover he slept with. Sitting up, he swung his legs over his bunk.

Thanks to Sharon's last minute request to compile all the departmental reports, he only got about four hours sleep. Each department was required to submit a status report for compilation on the ship as a whole. The exec normally performs the compilation of all the reports and presents to the captain for review. Sharon decided that is was time for Bill to learn to do them. It took him half the night. With a sigh, he stood up on the cool decking, stretched, and headed for the shower.

Bill's reflection in the mirror returned the image of a man in his late thirties with dark brown hair and brown eyes with a hint of green in them. A day's growth of stubble covered his normally clean-shaven jaw. Bill sported a mustache before he signed up for the Privateer. He had since shaved it off, but he still missed not having it. Facial hair could cause leaks in environmental masks when working on a planet that didn't support human life.

Freshly shaved, showered, and fully awake, Bill was ready to face the day. He pulled on underclothing before turning to the closet to pick out his attire. He selected a light blue shirt already fitted with the commander's bars on the collar. The left shoulder sleeve contained the crossed-rifle emblem of a weapons officer. His primary duty was to the five man crew that maintained and, when needed, fired the twin-barreled gun. The only firing they did on the Privateer was for practice. They also held secondary responsibilities as security personnel. They patrolled the ship in regular rotations to keep the peace among the crew. Tan colored slacks, black socks, black walking boots, and a black belt with a small silver buckle completed his attire. This was one of three different color schemes an officer of the merchant marines was authorized to wear. Although the merchant marines didn't enforce protocols with much vigor, the captains on each ship tended to. Many captains lived by the code that sloppy officers led to a sloppy crew.

Neatly dressed, Bill signed on to the display monitor to check for messages. He was relieved to see that Sharon had not rejected his summary reporting. He did receive a request for a supply overstock listing. This was being collected by the supply officer. He also needed to provide a listing of all broken or worn components that needed the attention of the repair facilities.

The last task Bill performed before logging off the computer was to see who was on watch in the weapons station and who was acting as a peace officer. He switched displays to see what the ship's status was. The last of the landing crew was back on board and the ship was roughly sixty eight thousand kilometers from the planet. Calculating in his head, he was able to determine that the jump point was another two days out. It was normal operating procedure to clear all planets, moons, and gravity wells before attempting to enter light speed.

Bill was in a fairly good mood as he left his cabin and headed towards the mess hall. He always looked forward to returning to Rap-3 after a setup was completed. Within a few days of docking, most of his crew would have departed to points unknown. His responsibility would be limited to the creation of daily reports. Most of these reports were made up of ship repairs, supply handling, and personnel movement. Once the remaining supplies were offloaded and the crew was gone, Bill's requirements on board the ship reduced greatly. Bill was usually mentally drained by the time he reached the docking station, so the reduction in responsibilities was always welcomed. With the refit scheduled this time around, Bill could look forward to being released from ship's duty for a while.

The mess hall on board the Privateer was small, so the crew ate in shifts. Bill had become used to eating with the fellow officers that appeared between each of his shifts. He knew that the overall spirit throughout the ship would be lifted this morning with the beginning of the voyage home. For Bill, home was a small two room inner cabin on the station. He was thinking that, once the ship was docked and he was finally released from ship's duty, he would head down to the planet Rapitine to do some hiking. Being in a quiet, peaceful area alone sounded great now. Rapitine had only been colonized in the past seventeen years, so most of its surface was uninhabited. Bill knew that this would remain as such for many years to come. Population growth on these outer colonies was slow due to a lack of influx of people with a desire to stick around.

Stepping into the mess hall, Bill headed for the serving line. Scrambled eggs, greasy bacon and sausages, along with French toast were the major features for this meal. Bill looked at the scrambled eggs and decided they were too watery for his taste. He ordered a ham and cheese omelet instead. He silently blessed the person who invented sterilized sealed containers. Fresh food kept long cruises manageable over that earlier processed crap he used to eat.

Vacuum-sealed shipping containers went a long way in prolonging food, but it wasn't until the introduction of sterilized mucus that the problem of food storage was solved. This sterile mucus was injected into the vacuum-sealed containers surrounding the food item, thereby causing stases to occur between the food item and any bacteria that it contained. Once the mucus was drawn back out, the food item was in the same condition as when it was stored. Bill thought about how gross that sounded. He decided it was better not to think about it.

The cook handing Bill a plate with his omelet on it brought him out of his thoughts. Adding three slices of bacon and a couple slices of French toast topped off his meal. Looking around as he poured syrup on the toast, he looked for a place to sit. He headed over to his usual table while trying to keep the syrup away from his omelet. Lieutenants Andrea Sloan and Rebecca Ladd already occupied two of the seats. The two were hunched over the table holding a quiet conversation. He thought about heading for another table in case they wanted their privacy, but Andrea looked up and waved him over. While sitting down, Bill noticed two of his weapons specialists already eating at another table. They were also getting ready to go on watch for this shift.

Andrea, as the engineering officer, oversaw a group of sixteen engineering specialists. She was tasked with keeping the Privateer in running order. She was also responsible for all of the equipment needed within the environmental buildings once they were constructed. Andrea and her crew were always among the busiest regardless of whether the ship was in route or orbiting a planet. She stood on a five foot nine inch frame and sported a muscular build common with engineers who labored over heavy equipment. Her eyes were dark brown and she wore her light brown hair at shoulder length. To Bill, she appeared to be in her mid-thirties. Like Bill, she was also wearing the blue and tan officer's uniform.

Rebecca worked as the transportation officer. She was responsible for all shuttle service to and from the ship as well as maintenance on the small crafts. Her crew of six was kept busy shuttling supplies to and from the ship, along with performing upkeep on docked shuttles. Her shuttles put in many hours of service and were sorely missed if any one of them broke down. Rebecca was a short woman at only five foot two and very thin. She preferred to keep her dirty-blond hair at collar length. Her stunning blue eyes could look right through you at times. Bill was always impressed with her maturity, which seemed to go beyond her young age. She was wearing the alternative uniform of a yellow blouse with dark blue slacks.

"Good morning, Andrea, Rebecca. You two seem to be busy conjuring up some rumor or other," Bill commented, then continuing without waiting for a reply. "I suppose you two are looking forward to getting back to civilization again."

Andrea replied, "You bet we are. The first thing I am going to do is take a long, hot bubble bath. Then I am going to spend several days just catching up on all the design changes in the clothing shops. It will sure be nice to shed these tiring uniforms."

Rebecca chimed in, "My first order of business is to head out for some real cooking. I have been dying for fresh seafood for months now. Then I will top that off with a large piece of chocolate cake with vanilla ice cream melting under a layer of hot fudge. Now that's what I call living."

Both women started chuckling to themselves. Rebecca asked, "How about you, Commander? Do you have any plans?"

Bill replied, "Well, after I settle in, I am thinking of taking a shuttle planet-side and doing some serious deep woods hiking and camping. One of the nicest things about Rapitine is its endless wooded areas. You can haul in about two weeks worth of supplies and lose yourself for a while. However, it does take a while to get used to the heavier gravity on that planet."

"Have a problem with hanging around us boring stiffs, Commander? I thought you found us stimulating? Are you turning hermit on us?" Andrea joked.

Deciding that was a question better left unanswered, Bill concentrated on his meal. Changing insults with these two quick-wits was a losing battle. Then, he remembered the transmission that had passed through the bridge yesterday. "Word has it that they will be upgrading the shuttles when we return. The company is supposed to have received some kind of deal on the Mark Seven models now that the Eight's are out. Think you can handle them, Lieutenant?"

Bill smiled as Andrea rolled her eyes. Rebecca's eyes, however, lit up, and Bill almost thought he could see her ears perk up. She started firing off questions: "Where did you hear that? Are you sure they were Mark Sevens? If you're playing with me, I'll have you ejected into space the next time you take a shuttle. Did you really hear that? Hell, I could pilot a Seven with my eyes close. What an improvement they would be over these old Fours we have. Each of them Sevens could haul twice what our Fours do now. Course, we would have to redesign the hangers to handle the larger crafts. The deck clamps won't line up with their support skids either. The inner and outer bay doors are too close together to handle the longer crafts. The Fours barely fit between them now. I wonder if the yard has thought of that retrofit yet."

Andrea couldn't stand it any longer. Talking to Rebecca about anything that could be flown was just asking for a long, boring conversation. Shaking her head, she said.

"Come on, Rebecca, you know that he was just pulling your leg. The company isn't going to get rid of these shuttles if they think they can get their money's worth out of them. Besides, how are you going to fit the Sevens into the shuttle bays when the Fours hardly fit now?"

Bill just smiled and started eating again. He wasn't kidding, but he was not going to let them off the hook that easily. He was on the bridge when the transmission came in to be prepared to offload the Fours. He would have loved to see the expression on the captain's face where she read it. He finally looked up to see both women staring at him waiting for a reply. He set his fork down while swallowing the last of his omelet. Picking up a slice of bacon, he said, "It is true, but I am not the one who should be telling you this. I was on the bridge when the message came in. The station workers want the shuttles to be offloaded, with all remaining parts, first thing upon our arrival. The Sevens are supposed to be loaded with spares and ready to send out to us. The captain has the message now, so you should be hearing about this soon. Don't say you heard this from me or this is the last time I share information with you two."

Bill wouldn't have been surprised if Rebecca had known about this already. Trying to keep a secret on any ship was nearly impossible. Usually, any noteworthy information spread around the ship before it could be officially announced. If someone could figure out how to travel space as fast as word spread around a ship, they could be home in days rather than weeks. Bill's thoughts were interrupted when Ensign Ein Zimmerman walked in. He glanced over at him while taking a bite of his bacon. Andrea and Rebecca had started a conversation about the configuration of the hanger bay and how it could be set up to handle the larger crafts. Rebecca was outlining the bay's configuration on a napkin.

Ein, the supply officer, was a tall black man standing six foot six and weighing about two hundred ninety pounds. With his very short hair and black eyes, he was an imposing figure. Ein was well known for being very stingy with handing over replacement parts. When you asked for a part, it helped to show him the worn out one first, as he was not likely to hand it over easily. A ship could only carry so much supplies and replacement parts. It was always in the crew's best interest to repair a part if possible rather than replace it too soon. Ein had a reputation as a wizard when it came to reusing worn or broken parts, a skill he was trying to pass on to the three others who reported to him.

At fifty-three, his days as a crew member were winding down. Having saved enough credits to retire, he was looking forward to returning home and settling down. Bill had heard that Ein had not been home in over fifteen years. This made Bill wonder if so much would have changed over that time span that Ein would not be comfortable there. Ein was one of the few who had made the transition from crew to officer core instead of being a product of an officer training program. As the guild and merchant marines grew, they were snatching up officers faster than the schools could push them out. Ein benefited from that officer shortage when he was a parts specialist for a number of years with the guild. He was coaxed away by the merchant marines with the offer of an officer's title.

Bill jerked his head towards Ein. "This will probably be the only time you'll be able to pull parts for the Mark Fours without a fight when he gets word to hand them over."

Rebecca smiled as she looked at Ein. "You're probably right. But, how much you wanna bet that he will make me sign for every blessed part he hands me? Maybe I'll just hook him up with the supply folks at the station since they talk the same language. I just might save myself a migraine in the process."

Ein walked over with a heaping plate that would have fed the other three combined. Grabbing the salt and pepper, he nodded to each in turn. "Good thing we're headin' back today. Runnin' out of most everything. Didn't expect to be gone no eight months. Ya think those knotheads back home would have figured that this planet was too hostile to put up a station very fast. They kept tellin' me we didn't need all I was askin' for."

Bill thought that the amount of food the supply officer had piled on his plate didn't support his concerns. Looking up at Ein, he said, "I'm sure it isn't that bad. They usually figure these things out so we don't come back with a whole lot of supplies left over. With the crew being so anxious to get away, they don't like to keep them aboard handling oversupply any more than they have to."

Ein stopped eating and looked over at Bill. "You'll sing a different tune when the coffee runs out. Ways I figure it, we have enough for another twenty-four days. Ever see the captain when she doesn't get her mornin' coffee? You know who they'll blame, don'tcha? Me! They'll say I shouldn't have given back what we had left over last time. But, hell, they empty everything befores they start overhaulin'. Do they expect me to stuff it in my pockets and keep it in those cheap ass living spaces? Can't hardly fit myself into one."

"You could tell the cooks to try mixing in half new with half used grounds and see if anyone notices the difference. Given the alternative, they may want to give it a try. I, for one, would not want to face the captain when she is suffering from caffeine withdrawal," Bill said jokingly.

"Humph," was all Ein said as he shook his head to show his disapproval before returning to his breakfast. He then froze with his fork halfway between his plate and mouth.

His eyes narrowed as he looked at the cooks with an evil grin. "You know, that ain't a bad idea," he said as he looked over at the steward refilling one of the large coffee urns. The contents of his fork spilled back onto his plate. "Just might be worth tryin'. Course, you have to be careful about how you ask them cooks how to fix something. They sure do get touchy on ya." Ein frowned as he put the empty fork into his mouth, only to discover no food came with it.

Andrea looked across at Bill and smiled. Bill could only hope that the cooks would dismiss the idea of mixing coffee grounds. He hoped the cooks would just lessen the amount of grounds they used per pot. He finished the last of his breakfast and coffee, which tasted a little better at the moment, and headed over for a refill. "I have to make my rounds before duty calls," he said over his shoulder as he filled his coffee cup.

Back in the walkway and heading aft, Bill knew he had about twenty minutes to check on his staff before heading to the bridge to take over as officer of the day. Entering one of the four turbo lifts, he selected deck one, aft twenty. This took him up from deck six and aft, stopping between compartments twenty-five and twenty-six. Stepping out of the lift, he walked forward to compartment twenty. The label on the hatch read 'Weapons Control Room'. This compartment was located directly under the gun turret. As Bill walked in, he spotted a single specialist leaning back in his chair with his feet on the console reading a book. The panels and displays at his feet were used to operate the turret, fire the guns, and monitor energy outputs from the plasma generators and capacitors. In the middle of the compartment, two round cylinders ran from the floor to the ceiling. Inside each cylinder was a series of conduits that carried the energy burst from the capacitors, which pulled energy from the plasma generators located several decks below. With the two he had seen eating breakfast,

THE KRRACTS ENCOUNTER

one making rounds and another probably sleeping off the last watch, that left this one to oversee this station. As soon as the two specialists finished eating breakfast, one would take over here while the other took over the roving watch. The specialist was peeking over the top of his book at his commander. He said, "Good morning, Commander. Sleep well?"

Bill walked over to the main console to look over the display screens. He said, "Not bad, Don. Of course it could have been longer. Looks like everything is in order. Any problems I should know about before I head off to the bridge?"

The weapons specialist, Don Bulloch, laid his book face down on the console and answered, "No problems, Commander. Everything is quiet so far. Both capacitors are fully charged with the generators on standby. The turret and fire controls are locked. Tracking defaulted to passive."

Bill glanced over at the target display to validate the control lock. This lock prevented anyone from operating the weapon controls. The captain, first officer, and Bill were the only ones who knew the code to unlock it. The lock could be released from the bridge where one of the three was always on duty. Bill could also override the control lock from this station. Once the lock was released, anyone attempting to use the weapon without orders could be locked out again from the bridge.

"Are you ready to go home?" Bill asked as he looked over each of the displays and validated that everything was working within tolerable limits. He also glanced at the book title that his specialist was reading. Bill tolerated reading on this watch because there was little a specialist could do outside of checking the status displays while the gun controls were locked. Being computer-controlled, a warning would sound if any monitor registered an anomaly in the readings. He felt it was better to have an alert specialist reading than a bored one nodding off.

"Yep, and with the credits I have coming from this mission I can have a pretty good time. Of course, that would be if the RAP stations and Rapitine had much to offer these days. I'm sure there have been a fair number of new releases out that I can go and see. Perhaps do a little gambling even though that casino they have is a big rip-off joint. I usually only hit the slots to waste time when I'm bored. But I can stock up on books, music and shows to take out on the next mission."

Bill looked at the time display on the wall above the console. It was 0745. He needed to be on his way up to the bridge. Nodding his head towards the book, he asked, "Didn't you read *The Rounded Square* before?"

"Yep, but I ran out of things to read a month ago, so I started reading them over again," Don replied.

"Well, I am due on the bridge. The breakfast tastes pretty good this morning, so enjoy. Oh, by the way, enjoy the coffee today; it may not taste as good tomorrow." Bill smiled to himself as he noticed the confused look on Don's face. He headed out without clarifying the comment. Returning to the lift, he requested the bridge. He had to enter his access code before the request would be honored. Only key personnel were allowed on the bridge when the ship was underway. The last thing any bridge officer wanted to see was a stir-crazy crew member running into the bridge with a fire ax or some other device.

The turbo lift doors swung open providing Bill with an angled view of the bridge. In the middle of the bridge was a half-circle ring of two-inch brass tubing that separated a set of captain's chairs from the raised outer walkway. The brass came to Bill's belt buckle in height. The ends of each side of the brass tubing curled inward into an eighteen-centimeter hole where the tubing formed a circle. Bill was always tempted to stick a flowerpot in each hole as a joke. Each side of the walkway ended at a set of steps. The forward bridge area was fourteen inches lower than the upper section. Once on the lower section, an inward turn brought you to the two captain's chairs. These slightly rotating simulated leather chairs were reserved for the captain, when she was on the bridge, and the first officer. When neither was on the bridge, the officer of the day would use one of these chairs during his or her watch. The captain's chairs overlooked the two command control consoles. The command consoles were positioned at forty-five degree opposing angles to one another, with enough room between them to allow passage to the foremost bridge area. The left console housed navigation while the right console was used for tracking. A specialist was seated at each station as required whenever the ship was in motion.

The navigational specialist handled all course changes and the ship's speed. This also included the command entries for jumping in and out of warp. While navigation handled the course selection, the tracking station monitored the ship's progress. Located against the bulkhead to the left of the lift was the scanning station. This station received input from the two sensor arrays. This station had a specialist at all times, except when the ship was docked.

Bill walked over to this station to observe the status of the arrays. He then started his walk around the railing, passing the lift again on his way to the communication station. A specialist monitored this station at all times. Communications concerning ship or mission status were routed to the ship's log for recording. With the first officer present at this station, Bill moved on.

The third and final upper station Bill came to was the damage control display station. Two display boards were located on the bulkhead above the station console. Each of these display boards was directly linked to damage control central, which was located deep within the ship. The larger, horizontal display board depicted a two-dimensional crosscut view of the ship. The crosscut display had lights located within each compartment. All the lights were currently showing green depicting normal status. A second smaller vertical display showed sensors, shielding, weapons, and other vital system status.

Once Bill had completed his rounds around the bridge, he paused to lean against the railing. He ran his hands over the smooth, cool surface of the rail as he scanned the various movements about the bridge.

Commander Sharon Bresee continued to look over the shoulder of a communications specialist. This usually signified that an incoming message was being received from the company as a final farewell message before they entered warp. The captain would have already sent the company a message updating them on the latest status of the environmental setup. This incoming message was probably from the company.

The Privateer used the latest tight-beamed pulsating light stream for communication. Messages relayed between two points required that both the sender and receiver's location be known in order for a message to be properly routed.

The distance of the Privateer from the space station required sixteen hours for a message to reach its destination. Tight-beam communication was reserved for long range communication. Communication between close objects still used sound frequencies. Technology was not available yet to communicate with a ship in warp.

Bill had seen enough of these messages to be able to read it without looking. It would say 'well done' to the ship and crew and 'have a safe journey home'. It would also contain the entry vector for coming out of warp close to the Rapitine planet and the docking station. They would also receive a timeline for when they were to exit warp. This allowed the station traffic monitors to prevent other ships from being within this exit point when the Privateer arrived. Should the ship be early or late, the captain was required to exit warp at the system's edge. They would have to stay at that location until they received a new entry vector. This could add hours to their travel time if traffic around the station was heavy that day. Navigators were very careful to insure that a ship arrived within its expected time.

Bill would not interrupt Sharon while she was working with the communication specialist. All crew members held a specialist title for their area of expertise. Bill held sixteen specialist titles on his way to receiving a pilot certificate. Without that certificate, he could not be a bridge officer. Sharon broke through his thoughts when she said, "Hello, Bill. I take it you are ready to relieve me? Everything is in order. We are on course for our exit point at standard half speed. All status indicators are green. I am waiting until this incoming message is converted so I can take it to the captain. How are you holding up?"

As the second in command, Sharon was responsible for the logistical task needed to run the Privateer. She carried several labels like first officer, executive officer, number one, exec or just XO. Regardless of the title, her job was to free up the captain from having to deal with the day-to-day activities of the crew. At six feet tall, she looked more than capable of handling anything that could arise. Sharon was from a mix of white and Oriental parents. The Oriental characteristics showed in her face and short black hair. Her lighter complexion and tall features reflected the other. Bill liked Sharon even though she seemed to dump a lot of duties onto him. During this mission, Bill had learned more from her about running a ship than he thought possible. Bill had come to learn just about everything that he needed to know to handle the Privateer. Whether this was

Sharon's goal or some other hidden meaning, he hadn't quite figured out yet. He was leaning towards the latter because he seemed to be learning by trial and error.

Bill responded, "Not bad considering how long this setup took. I am looking forward to some relaxation when we get back. Do you still think you will be able to meet up with Thomas now?"

"I am hoping to be able to catch a transport over to New Rodell to see if I can catch up with him. Last I heard his ship was scheduled for a lengthy stay there. With any luck it will still be around when we dock. I haven't really given it much thought past that."

Sharon had an on-again, off-again relationship with another officer known to him only as Thomas. He was the new executive officer of a transport ship. Bill suspected that, when Sharon became captain of a vessel, she would recruit Thomas as the exec to allow them to be together. Sharon didn't talk much about him or their relationship. But she sure seemed fixated on the Privateers return trip home.

"Message is ready, Commander," the communication's specialist said without turning around.

Sharon pulled a pocket recorder from its carrying case attached to the side of her brown slacks. She lightly slapped the device into the palm of the specialist's hand. The specialist plugged in the recorder and copied the transmission onto it. A soft beep indicated that the computer had completed the transfer. Taking back the recorder, Sharon walked around the rail to sit in one of the captain's chairs. Bill followed and slid into the chair next to her. Sharon was already reading the message from the lighted display on top of the recorder. Her expression did not change, but Bill could sense that the message was not sitting well with her. After a few minutes, she handed the recorder to Bill. Bill reset the message to start over:

ATD: 1541; Date: 2246; From: CEO Ernest T. Leander; Validation: ADM Wilson Swensen; Message as follows:
Confirmation received on success of installation of latest habitat; congratulations to all; Rescind orders returning to Orbiter Rap-3; highest priority to divert to alternative location; mission to locate and validate status of probe 13-115-98; probe lost on return from 686.93880.223; stop at jump point and set navigation point to arrive at estimated point of lost probe; retrieve if feasible; else determine fate and report; wait reply; message ended;

Bill handed the recorder back to Sharon while looking her in the eyes. In a low voice that only Bill could hear, she said, "This is not going to sit well with the captain or the crew. I should take the cowards way out by delegating you to take it to her. Then you can listen to the tirade I am pretty sure she will go into." She paused for a few seconds as if thinking about doing just that. "I am pretty sure this will blow any chance I had of meeting up with Thomas. If I'm not back in thirty minutes, send a rescue party, will you?" Standing up, she headed for the upper walkway and said for all to hear, "Commander Launtra has the bridge." She then disappeared into the lift, recorder in hand, ready to present the bad news to the captain.

Bill sat and stared out at the images projected on the main view screen. For a moment there he really thought Sharon was going to hand this one off to time. He knew this would not sit well with the crew because they were mentally prepared to go back home. The captain will split a conduit when she reads the message, Bill thought. Was the information in that probe worth more than the sanity of the crew? It was apparent that the company thought it was. Bill was surprised that the authorities from the merchant marines let them have the extra time. The Privateer had completed five straight missions without a refit. The engines were getting tired, and structural fatigue was always a problem. Were they tempting fate? The Privateer had not experienced any serious problems so far, and she had plenty of spare parts on hand, but how much wear could she take before she started breaking down at just the wrong time? Bill noticed that the crew members on the bridge were looking at him. They were trying to gauge the importance of the message by his reaction to it. He knew better than to ignore that concern. Bill quickly tried to come up with something to say that would prevent the start of the rumor mill. It was fortunate for Bill that the Privateer was coming up on the largest of the moons orbiting this planet. "Look at the colors within that moon. If I had half a brain, I would take up painting and make a fortune selling it to the orbit-lubbers back home." Bill could hear the chuckles from the crew around him as they returned to their duties.

Bill leaned back in his chair thankful that he was not the exec just now...

chapter three

After ordering Brk'erst to take the ship over to the tracking buoy to transfer all data onto the ship's computers, sysnka byf stormed off the bridge. He had also ordered brk'erst to replace the buoy with the upgraded models they carried. With this completed they were under way again to take up station farther away from the planet. Brk'erst now waited for the overlord to return.

Overling v'sdntil was trying hard not the let his frustration show. The tan hide running down the back of his head was beginning to redden. The krracts had a light tan colored hide covering their body to help with living in the hot climate of their planet. Blood vessels ran close to small vent holes in the hide for releasing heat. When a krracts became heated, blood would route through these vessels to allow it to cool through the vented hide. The blood running through these vessels would cause the hide to pick up a reddish hue. V'sdntil's body temperature was rising as his frustration mounted. He had run through the buoy's tracking data about a dozen times, but he was still unsure what the object's mission was. He also ran through the ship's tracking data from when they entered the system until the object was destroyed. He was hoping that the reaction from the object would provide some clues as to its intent.

Pressing another display key brought up the buoy's tracking data. He had transferred the memory over from the tracking buoy several dozen beat cycles ago.

He played the readout again, selecting to run one beat equal to one hundred beats in time. It showed a small metallic object entering the system. It had selected a specific planet and proceeded into an orbit around it. He noticed that it selected an orbit opposite of the planet's rotation. He wondered if that meant anything. He guessed that if you wanted to speed up the time it took to go around a planet, that would be the best way. After eleven rotations, v'sdntil counting each one, the object exited orbit to head back out again. It gave every impression that it was studying that specific planet. The krracts had been to these planets before, only to find them worthless.

Altering the display he read the data from the targeting computer. Amazing was all that v'sdntil could think as he watched. He wondered how an object that small could have shielding that effective. He wondered what kind of technology the species that owned the object must be capable of. He did not like the thought of having to find out. It was clear that the object did not make it through that concentrated blast. This gave him some satisfaction. At least the object did not appear to be too intelligent.

V'sdntil sighed again. He was not aware of how loud it had become. Once again, he reviewed the tracking data. He concentrated on the buoy's readouts. The answer must be there, somewhere. He was getting hungry, too, but he did not want to risk leaving his station until he could provide the overlord with a reasonable answer as to what the object was doing here. He liked being an overling, so he had no desire to give the overlord a reason to demote him back to underling. V'sdntil sighed once more before concentrating even harder on the recordings.

Looking in the direction of the sound of the sighing, brk'erst knew what was bothering the overling. He had the same concerns. The overlord would want answers to provide to the Council. The Council had little tolerance for failures in carrying out a directive.

Overlord synska byf paced around his living space. He was still fuming over the incident with the object. It was probably a tracking vessel of some kind, he thought. Was it ahead of an advancing force? Was it some kind of pre-invasion search? Whose was it and where did it come from? He was sure that he should have taken more time to think things through before reacting to the situation. But, then again, he was passing by the object at an alarming rate of speed. If he had waited too long to decide what to do, the object would have exited the system. He was sure that letting that object escape would have been a far worse fate. Whatever its purpose was, the opportunity to find out was lost. So was the information it contained. On the plus side, the communication overling had not picked up any transmitted signals before the object was destroyed.

Walking over to his small desk, he sat down in front of the monitor. Thinking the message over in his head, he recorded his report for the Council. Satisfied with the context, he sent it. Calculating in his head, he knew that the earliest that he could expect an answer was in about four hundred beat cycles. He paced around his living space for a while longer before finally sitting down. Sometimes, he wondered why he ever wanted to command a ship.

Synska byf was a loyal follower of the krracts society and beliefs. He did not question the orders he received from the Council nor did he feel the need to complain about his assignments. Being a krracts made him, by nature, impatient and somewhat paranoid. He matured during the drive to reach beyond their planet, causing him to be constantly assigned to a ship. Although he knew that his role did not have the status that it once did, this was what he was trained to do. He had hoped to be commanding a destroyer or cruiser some day, but that looked like an empty dream now. With the fleet docked at home, the need for command overlords evaporated. He also wondered how long it would be before the Council decided to abandon space altogether. He had been traveling in space for a long time and had yet to see anything to make him believe that another species existed. Except for today, he reminded himself. Could this change everything? He had seen an object small enough to be placed into the storage hold of his ship, which appeared to have superior technology to anything the krracts had. If the makers of that object had ships, it was a good assumption that they would be of a far superior design than any of the krracts ships. They would most likely just fly right on through any fleet the Council tried to round up to stop it. That was assuming they could find enough experienced krracts to crew the ships. He could only think of a handful of overlords still living who could command a ship. An inexperienced crew on a ship that could be inferior to an enemy was not a good combination to have while defending your planet. He wondered if the Council had these same thoughts. He doubted it, as they seemed to have altered their focus away from space. However, this just might have changed their thinking.

Similar thoughts ran through his head as he got up and paced again. He had lost all track of time when a signal from the console snapped him out of his thoughts. He walked over to the desk and sat before the monitor again. He hesitated for a few beats before playing the return response from the Council.

"Overlord synska byf, the Council members have reviewed your report. Transfer to the Council all data relating to this incident from both your ship and the tracking buoy. You are ordered to stay at your current location to monitor for any further activities. You will remain on station until you receive

further orders. Use whatever caution is necessary to avoid contact with any other objects that may enter the system. By order of Council member Overlord Iridnijg sli."

Further activities? The overlord wondered if the Council was anticipating more activity in this area. Then he realized that the Council was having him stay on station here. He surmised this meant that they were not displeased with his performance after all. He was sure they would have preferred to have the object, but it appeared they were not questioning his actions leading up to destroying it. At least for now, he cautioned himself. But, it disturbed him that they did not mention any support being sent. He would expect them to at least send another ship out for support. Even another minelayer would be welcomed at the moment. He hoped they were rounding up a crew to get at least one warship ready just in case. His little minelayer would not be much of a deterrent if a fleet of ships were to suddenly pop into the system. In fact, he doubted if his ship would be much of a match for a single warship, based on the technology he had seen so far. Having a cruiser or two to hide behind would suit him just fine. He wondered if he should request permission to lay a minefield out where he would expect a ship to appear, but he decided against this, knowing that the Council knew the capability of his ship and would have ordered the mining if they deemed it necessary. Closing the Council message, he paged the bridge.

When brk'erst responded to the page, the overlord ordered, "We have been ordered to remain here. Set up a connection with the buoy, then plot a course for the second planet. Place the ship in a position to allow the planet to shield us against discovery using the entry and exit vectors of the object. We will use the buoy's sensor to monitor the areas we can't see. Also, have the communication overling transmit all the tracking data from the buoy, along with the targeting data from our ship, to the Council. Any questions, underlord?"

"No, Overlord. Your order is understood and will be carried out at once," brk'erst replied.

The overlord knew the underlord would take care of what needed to be done. If there was a ship or two about to pop into the system, he wanted to be in position to report back and ask for support. He was not about to be sitting out here exposed should that happen. Being hidden behind a planet would give him an advantage while also keeping his ship out of harm's way. If he was able to provide the Council with enough advanced warning of an invasion, it would be well-remembered later when considering him for a sli title.

The sli title was the highest ranking a krracts could achieve. Most krracts never receive the ranking of a sli even after becoming a byf. Some died in fights disputing claims to females, while others would die stalking prey. Some of the prey could be just as deadly as the krracts that stalked them. Mostly, though, it was a bad decision as a byf that sinks any hope of reaching the sli level. An overlord, having reached a byf level, was expected to make sound decisions. Making a decision that is seen later by the Council to be questionable, would place a black mark on the overlord and sink his chances for consideration of a sli title. Without the sli title, an overlord had no hope of becoming a Council member. The krracts mentality didn't understand failure. A downhearted male just lost his desire to live and usually died within a few weeks. Female krracts detecting the loss of a male's drive would abandon the ghugg, leaving the male to dive deeper into despair.

Synska byf sat down on his hammock. He looked over at the monitor to see how his orders were being carried out. He could feel the ship altering course back to the buoy. He knew that they would have to retrieve the buoy and install a tight beam transmitter to allow for a better link between his ship and the buoy. It would take a while to fix up the buoy before they could even set course for the other planet. He was going to take this opportunity to rest up. The overlord had decided that once he was rested and the ship returned to a regular routine, he would begin rotating bridge duties with his underlord. He wanted to remain sharp in case something unexpected occurred. He reached up and turned on the overhead heat lamps. The warming from the heat was making him relax even more. He was soon fast asleep.

chapter four

Captain Linda Eccles was sitting behind her desk staring at the report she was writing. She was trying to come up with just the right words that would help her get her exec reassigned when the Privateer returned. To Linda, Sharon was a waste of breathable air. She had grown tired of listening to her gripes about delays in the Privateer's return to port, and how it would ruin her chances to meet up with Thomas, whoever the hell he was.

Linda could size up Sharon in three words, "She was lazy." It was as simple as that. Sharon did as little work as possible and had a great knack of passing off work onto others. The person who took the most brunt of this was Bill. Oh, Sharon thought she was clever about it, but Linda knew what was going on. However, Linda was taking advantage of the situation. She wanted Bill as her exec, but Bill needed more line experience in running the day-to-day operations of the ship. Sharon, in her laziness, was providing Bill with that valuable experience. And who was Linda to interfere with such affairs. Linda smiled at that thought. She knew she was taking advantage of the situation, but hell, that was captain's prerogative right?

Now, what to do with Sharon, the real problem at hand? She hated to get her assigned as another exec and become a burden on another captain. If she could write it just so, perhaps the company would give her command of a smaller vessel. As captain, she could delegate all she wanted. Perhaps if she wrote it just right, the guild would steal her away, and it would serve them right. She had never been a fan of the overbearing guild.

Sharon waited outside the captain's cabin to gather her thoughts. The door was closed, so she did not have to worry about being seen. Mentally ready, she did a quick check of herself to make sure she was presentable. She then gave the door three loud knocks. She waited for the captain to invite her in.

"Enter," Linda said without bothering to look up. She saved the report and closed it down. She made Sharon wait for her to complete her task before recognizing her presence. It was her prerogative to make others wait until she was of a mind to receive them. Finally glancing up, she looked Sharon up and down. She noted the recorder in Sharon's hand. "I read over the daily reports. Did you write them?"

Linda could see that Sharon was caught between answers. She had to decide if she would say she wrote them, in case they were good, or say Bill did them in case they were bad. What to do, what to do? Linda was loving the conflict she was putting Sharon's mind through. Finally, Sharon responded, "Actually, I worked with Bill on them. I thought he could use the experience."

Not bad, a nice safe answer. Linda could almost applaud Sharon for her creativity and ability to think quickly on her feet. Linda responded, "I see from the reports that we are seriously low on stores, supplies and fuel for the shuttles. Timing could not be better to be heading back."

"Captain, I have some bad news for you. I have here," Sharon placed the recorder in Linda's hand, "A return reply from the company. They are asking us to take a detour."

Linda reached out to take the recorder, then stopped. "What do you mean a detour? They must know that our food stores are calculated to only last the number of days they estimate we will be gone. Damn idiots!" She snatched the recorder out of Sharon's hand. Sharon remained silent as she waited for Linda to read it. She could see Linda's cheeks reddening slightly as she neared the end. She was beginning to think that having Bill standing here instead of her would have been the better part of valor.

Finished, Linda said, "Someone must really have their head in a vacuum to come up with these orders. They have an entire fleet of warships sitting around collecting space dust. Do they use them? No! They ask us to go gallivanting through space looking for a probe that most likely has a busted transmitter. How much do you want to bet the probe will arrive back at the spaceport about the time we arrive where they think it is? Damn company's focus on the bottom line is going to give me an ulcer one of these days."

As the captain vented her frustration, Sharon listened patiently. She didn't like the orders any better than Linda did. It would mean the Privateer would be that much later getting back. It seemed like the entire universe stood between her and Thomas. When Linda stopped talking, she said, "You want me to handle the course change?"

"No, I had better let the crew know first or we may have a mutiny on our hands when word of this get outs. We bust our butts to get the environmental setup completed on what has to be the most inhospitable planet I have ever encountered, and this is the thanks we get. We battled high winds, unstable surface movements, dust storms, lightning strikes…and for what? I don't know about you, but I think the crew has a right to be upset about these orders. Maybe you could start a mutiny and hijack us back to Rap-3. You can always declare insanity as a defense," Linda said, only half joking.

"Not me, thanks. Those maritime review boards can come down pretty hard on us mutineers. This might be a better job for Bill." Sharon could just picture Bill's face when he was asked to Shanghai the ship for home. She chuckled to herself.

Linda stood up and came around the desk. She slapped the recorder back to Sharon's open palm as she walked past. Another assignment for you to pass off to Bill, she thought. "No use stalling on this," she said as she walked out of her cabin. Sharon followed close behind. She heard the captain mutter, "Damn, but I hate that company at times."

When Bill heard the lift doors open, he came to his feet and observed Linda and Sharon entering the bridge together. Bill could see the sour expression on the captain's face. Just an inch shorter than Sharon, Linda sported cropped brown hair that reached her collar. Her matching brown eyes had a hard look to them at the moment. Her stride to the command chair was full of purpose. She was wearing the darker brown slacks that were usually favored by command officers like herself and Sharon. She had opted for the yellow shirt. Sharon, in contrast, was wearing the traditional light blue shirt.

"Mister Launtra, we are about to change course, if you will please," Linda said as she continued around the left side of the rail to the command chairs.

Bill stepped forward between the two command consoles to allow Sharon and Linda to take their seats. From this position, he would be able to monitor the changes as each specialist entered them.

"Mr. Launtra, I have the bridge. I would like to have your assistants with the navigational settings. Commander," Linda requested of Sharon, "I would like to have the navigational charts displayed, please." Linda had taken up the habit of calling Bill 'mister' as opposed to 'commander' to avoid confusion between him and Sharon when she gave orders. Sharon was senior to Bill, so she rated the commander title over Bill in the captain's mind. When giving orders, she preferred a short and direct approach in names. He was Mr. Launtra and Sharon was simply 'commander'. Orders can come fast and furious at times, and this helped to insure the correct person was acting on them. Normally, all three of them would seldom be on the bridge at the same time.

As the charts displayed on the forward monitor, Linda took a moment to review them. She then glanced down at Bill. "Mr. Launtra, set navigational headings for jump vector 686 mark 93880 mark 223. Compute course with minimal deviation. Jump speed will be warp four."

Bill repeated the order to the navigational crew. The information was already being entered into the system, and the results were being displayed on the screens at the stations on each side of him. Bill glanced over at the closest screen and repeated back the information. "Jump vector set for 686 mark 93880 mark 223, speed warp four, fastest track." He glanced at both screens before continuing with, "New jump point coordinates calculated and verified, Captain."

Acknowledging the order, Linda replied, "Very well, Mr. Launtra."

Bill watched as the captain pressed an activation key on the front of the armrest. This brought up a small command panel out of its resting place, along side her chair, to come to rest along side the right arm rest. Two tones were heard from the overhead speakers as Linda activated the com-unit. The captain began to speak.

"This is the captain to all crew members. I have received orders from the company for us to make a side trip before we head for home. I know that all of you were looking forward to a smooth trip back to civilization, but we have been asked to provide assistance to a misbehaving probe. Being that our job relies on the data from these probes, the company thought we might be interested in helping them retrieve it. We will be making a quick jump to see if we can find it, bring it aboard if possible, and then head home. It will take us approximately ninety-eight hours to reach the probe's last known location. I will see to it that the company adds an additional week's credits for each of you, and I will ask them to add another week's credit if we can bring the probe back home. I am sure some extra credits will come in handy at the cost of only a few days' delay, considering we will be in refit this time around. I would also like to take a moment to say well done to everyone for your efforts in completing the setup. I know this was one of the longer, more difficult setups we've encountered. The fact that it went smoothly reflects on the skills each of you bring. Make all preparations for entering light speed. Captain out." She pressed a key to return the panel to its stored position.

Sharon leaned over and asked, "Taking a little liberty with company funds?"

Linda replied, "I will insist on a little extra pay for this endeavor to make rescuers out of us. Besides, it's not like they can't afford it. Join me in a cup of coffee, Commander?"

Linda then left her chair saying, "Mr. Launtra, the bridge is all yours," as she headed into the lift with Sharon in tow.

The lift door closed and all was quiet again. Bill sighed and returned to one of the command chairs. He had a feeling that this quick side trip would delay them more than just a few days. As far as he knew, no probe had ever come up missing before. The company put a lot of money into that technology to make sure they were sturdy enough to survive space travel and smart enough to come home again. If it was missing out there, something nasty must have happened to it.

Thinking about the captain's order to use warp four, Bill wondered if she was trying to reduce stress to the drives.

Not a good sign, he thought. She must have been worried about the number of hours that were on the drive units since the last overhaul. He guessed it was better to be safe than sorry.

Linda and Sharon arrived in the mess hall to find it empty. The captain took up a mug and offered it to Sharon. She then took one herself and filled it with coffee. Leading the way to a table Linda said, "Sharon, there is something I would like to chat about. Now seems as good a time as any."

Once they were both seated Linda said, "I first wanted to say that I appreciate the work you have been doing on educating Bill." Sharon had a momentary look of panic in her eyes. Linda added, "Bill has a great wealth of experience in the service. He is going to make a great exec in the future. What you have worked with him on will go a long way to helping him get there." Sharon seemed to relax some.

Taking a sip of her coffee, Linda paused for a moment. Sharon seemed a little lost for words, so Linda continued, "Sharon, I think you have served your purpose onboard the Privateer. I am going to recommend you for command. While I think you have work to do yet to take on a command like the Privateer, you definitely have the skills to handle smaller assignments. Perhaps supply runs with a small freighter, or even ferry runs between colonies. Do you think you are ready to command your own ship?"

Sharon was still lost for words. Linda just sipped on her coffee and waiting for Sharon to put her thoughts together. Linda deliberately continued to wait, making the wait uncomfortable for Sharon. Sharon eventually responded, "I'm not sure what to say Captain. I feel confident that I can run my own crew. It is very gratifying to know that my hard work here has been recognized and rewarded."

Linda almost laughed in her face. She wanted so much to say, "Hard work my ass, the only hard work you had was trying to track Bill down to do your work for you." But she just smiled and said, "I am sure going to hate to lose you Sharon. But every bird has to fly off on their own eventually. It wouldn't be fair for me to keep you in the nest any longer." And I would probably have to kill you on the next trip, she thought.

Sharon was lost in her thoughts at the moment. Linda just couldn't stand to be around her any longer. She got up and said, "I have to get back to the reports due when we dock. If something comes to mind and you want to talk about it, just let me know."

It had been two work-cycles since v'sdntil had quit looking over the data recordings from the buoy and the ship. He was now relaxing over a treat of tweel worms. He kept his own supply, as did most of the crew, living in a box under his cot. V'sdntil fed these worms from meat scraps pilfered from his daily meal. This kept the worms fat and juicy—the only way any real krracts would eat them. These worms had been his favorite treat ever since he was a ling. Running his long claws through the dirt, he uprooted another worm. He quickly grabbed it behind the head with his other hand. It was a mature one about as long as his arm and as thick as his finger. He raised it over his head to allow the tail to be fed into his mouth. He slowly chewed it up as he fed it in. He was really enjoying the taste as fluid ran down his throat. The tweel worm was trying to burrow into v'sdntil's palm, but couldn't bite into the tough krracts' hide. V'sdntil had learned the painful lesson as a ling not to attempt to eat a tweel worm headfirst. Doing so was a race against who bit whom first. Placing the screened lid back on, he slid the box back into the relative darkness under the cot. He was due back on the bridge soon.

Overlord synska byf was pacing about the bridge. They were on their ninth crew rotation without any further incident. It was not in his nature to be patient. As a natural hunter, he preferred to be tracking his prey. This waiting game was not to his liking. To keep contact with the buoy and not be seen, the ship had been positioned alongside the second planet. The problem that the overlord had with this was that he could not communicate with the Council. His communication path was blocked by the same planet he was using to keep out of site of the entry point of the object. Currently, he was using the planet's rotation as a measurement in time. Each time the planet made a full revolution, they would race out the other side and check for incoming messages before returning to pick up the link with the buoy. This was frustrating as well as draining on both crew and ship. He wondered why the Council just didn't place a few more buoys out here and let him go home. He longed for the thrill of hunting down a fine meal.

It was nearing time for the underlord to arrive to relieve him. The overlord was looking forward to lying under the heat lamps again to take a warm nap. The krracts slept in short spurts throughout their cycles rather than taking a long sleep period. Synska byf looked up at the planet on the main view screen. The computer-generated marker was just beginning to show on the horizon. He knew that the underlord would have to make another trip out for a message check about halfway into his rotation on the bridge. However, this time, he was going to place a buoy out there so he could have it relay any messages to him without moving the ship back and forth. He shook his head when he thought about the wasted trips he had taken before the underlord had suggested this to him.

He knew that he should have thought of this. He shook his head over the wasted trips they have already made running back and forth.

Turning at the sound of the access door opening to the bridge, he expected to see brk'erst, but it was just a tracking overling getting ready to take over at his position. Synska byf returned to his pacing. Again, he glanced at the planet where the marker was now clearly visible on this side of the horizon. He resumed his pacing that had stopped while contemplating his thoughts.

"Sorry for the interruption, Overlord, but the buoy has just detected a large object coming into the system. Possibly a ship, but it is too hard to tell at this distance. Would you like me to place it on the view screen?" the tracking overling asked.

Synska byf was at a loss for words for a few beats. He really didn't expect anything to happen out here while he waited for the word to continue with his duties. The sudden excitement was causing his digestive system to kick in. Could it really be a ship, perhaps it was only one of theirs sent out to relieve him? Yes, that was most likely what the buoy was seeing, he thought. Then he realized that the overling was still waiting for a reply.

He responded, "Yes. Transfer the current live feed over to the secondary viewer."

"As you command, overlord. The image is being transferred now," the overling answered. Once he had completed the transfer, he got up so v'sdntil could take over.

Unable to see anything on the live image, the overlord referred to the tracking display. The tracking display was showing an inbound object. The tracking calculations showed a reduction in speed characteristic to a braking ship. Since this braking reflected an unnatural slowing of the object, it could only be a powered vessel of some kind. As an afterthought, he asked v'sdntil to play back the buoy data from just prior to the object's arrival. When v'sdntil played it back, he could see the distant flash from the object coming out of light speed. This, plus the size calculated by the sensor, confirmed it had to be a ship.

The computer-displayed information being printed below the object's image was providing the overlord with little useful information. It was just too far away for any real identification. But, by the calculated mass though, it appeared to be larger than the bfnor torrnt. From the position the ship had arrived in, it was unlikely to be a krracts ship. He would have expected a krracts ship to come in above the third planet. This object had come in almost directly in line with the fourth planet. Dangerous, thought the overlord. If they had overshot their entry by even a beat they would have plowed directly into the planet itself. Whoever commanded that ship didn't seem too smart to synska byf.

More excitement swelled within synska byf because he knew he had made a good decision on where to place his ship. He was completely invisible with the planet being between him and them. The object would not be able to detect him just as he would not have been able to detect the object without the sensor from the buoy. He had a good advantage over whatever was out there. On the down side, though, the sensor was not as good as the one his ship carried. He would have to wait longer to get better information as the ship drew closer.

Synska byf didn't turn around when he heard the access door open again, but the heavy footsteps told him that the underlord was approaching. None of the overlings would make that heavy of a sound. He could also pick up the underlord's scent now. Without turning around, he said, "Underlord, we have an inbound object approaching. It is currently braking from its exit out of light speed. The tracking computer has it calculated at just slightly larger in mass than our ship. But that may be adjusted as the ship comes in closer."

"I doubt it is one of ours. The entry vector is too high. It is coming in close to where the other object came in at," brk'erst noted.

This observation impressed the overlord. Brk'erst continued, "So, are they here to retrieve the object we destroyed, or the advanced scout for a fleet? Either way, we are in a perfect position to watch what develops without risking ourselves. Unfortunately, it will be a long wait before the ship is close enough to make out clearly."

After a moment of silence, the overlord responded, "I think it may be too risky to lose contact with this ship now to send a message. We best wait and see if more ships arrive. I don't want to be blinded until I have a comfort level for what is happening here." If only I had that buoy in place to communicate with the Council directly, he thought.

Turning to look at his underlord, synska byf could see that brk'erst was wearing his normal attire. This included a wide black belt with a yellow cloth of the same width that ran from a clip in the belt at the left hip, across his chest to his right shoulder, and then across his back to meet at the clip again. The center of the belt contained a large, polished, metal buckle that had the bfnor torrnt stamped on it. The belt also contained three pouches that held devices that he used in his normal duties. Brk'erst wore no real clothing. Any clothing he could have worn would have interfered with his natural ability to release heat.

Krracts seldom wore clothing other than in a symbolic fashion. The belt was needed by brk'erst to carry items, and the yellow cloth was added for a symbol of status. Most overlings wore a similar belt and cloth combination, but did it using colors that identified their position. The bridge crew used a purple cloth with a symbol that identified the station they attended. Synska byf was wearing the red cloth reserved for overlords.

Synska byf noted that the underlord was beginning to show that muscular maturity needed to be considered for an overlord title. He figured that the underlord was perhaps another twelve solar cycles from reaching his full potential. Studying the underlord a little more, he could see that his fangs were nearly long enough now to disable even the largest of prey. He took a mental note to go out on the hunt with him when they got back. This would give him a real good perspective on the underlord's cunning and ferocity.

Turning his attention back to the tracking image, he started wondering what kind of vessel this was, what it looked like, and what kind of armament it had. He knew he was going to have a hard time sitting still and waiting. So far, no other ships had arrived behind it. He then wondered how much ahead of a fleet a scouting ship would normally be. He shook it off, as he figured it was most likely up to whoever made those decisions for that race of beings.

The incoming object was still too far away for the small buoy sensor to supply much useful information. The speed at which it traveled coming out of light speed allowed it to cover a sizable amount of distance before the braking was completed. The ship had reached a point where the light reflected off it. He could just pick it out over the stars beyond. The object was now under standard propulsion with a steady heading.

On a hunch, v'sdntil played back the trajectory the original small object had been traveling when they'd intercepted it. He then compared that with the direction of the oncoming ship. He was disappointed when the entry point of this ship did not match up to the smaller object. He would have expected the entry point to be the same if the object had been tracking ahead of this ship. He was also puzzled as to why the object had used a different exit point as compared to where it had entered into the system. The current course of this incoming ship was going to take it close by the point where the first object was destroyed. He wondered if this ship had the ability to detect any of the particles left behind in the explosion. The krracts sensors were not that sensitive, but he wondered if they were on this ship.

Having completed his conversation with the overlord, brk'erst was monitoring the work each overling performed at their stations. When he walked by the tracking station, he noticed that the small screen in front of the tracking overling contained a series of curved lines.

"What are you viewing, overling?" he asked.

"I am comparing the entry and exit headings from the first object, with the current heading of this ship. These two points will intersect at this location, Underlord." V'sdntil tapped the screen using a claw from one of his three long, tan fingers. His sharp black claw made a clicking sound as it touched the screen. He continued, "I was interested in seeing how this ship's enter into the system compared to where the other object entered and attempted to exit from. If two of the points matched, it would verify that the object and ship came from the same location. But, as you can see here, this ship arrived nearly sixteen degrees out system from the first object."

V'sdntil stopped his tapping as a trajectory change tone was heard. He quickly altered the tracking display to return to the live feed. The object was slowing down again. The ship appeared to be stopping close to the intersecting path with the first object.

"The tracking buoy is recording a change in the ship's speed. Rear propulsion emissions are decreasing. Braking thruster emissions are being detected," v'sdntil said.

Even though brk'erst was sure that synska byf had overheard the conversation between him and the overling, he repeated the overling's report. He then hurriedly continued his observations around the bridge to return to his overlord's side.

The overlord was studying the live image on the secondary viewer. It was still just a circle of light. He wondered why it had stopped. Had it detected something, maybe the buoy? He wondered if this would be a good time to break off contact and send a message to the Council. With any luck, he could be out and back before this ship started moving again. But what if it has stopped to wait for more ships to arrive? Once again, he realized that his lack of vision on setting up that second buoy was coming back to torment him. He was in a quandary as to what to do: stay and keep observing or risk it and hope for the best. He decided it was time to pace again.

Bill was back on duty as the Privateer was due to come out of warp. The captain and first officer had arrived on the bridge about ten minutes ago. Bill would have to leave soon because maritime law required a flight officer to be in emergency control when entering or exiting warp. The captain would order Bill to take up this position soon. From there, Bill could take over control of the bridge functions should something serious happen to the ship. Bill had already updated the captain on the ship's status. Now, it was just a matter of time before he was relieved.

"Mr. Launtra, I have the bridge. Please take up your station in emergency control. Report readiness when you arrive," the captain ordered as she handed him a security disc. The disc contained the code needed to override the ship's controls.

"Yes, Captain." Bill glanced at the exit countdown as he stepped into the lift. Knowing he had enough time for a quick detour, he headed for the cafeteria to pick up a pitcher of coffee and an armload of ready-made sandwiches. He was hungry, and it was a good bet those in the control room were as well. "A little preparation can go a long way," he said to himself.

Upon entering the control room, Bill placed the coffee and sandwiches on the counter. He then took a seat in front of the master control console and inserted the security disc. While the disc was being processed, he grabbed a sandwich for himself, as a hungry crew was quickly depleting the supply. Once the master control accepted the override code, he altered the override command status from inactive to stand-by. This would allow him to quickly take control of the ship, if need be. "Let's hope I don't need to," he mumbled.

Bill opened a channel to the bridge and reported, "Bridge, this is Commander Launtra. Please notify the captain that I have assumed command in emergency control. Override command status is in stand-by, station fully crewed and ready."

Sharon responded, "Emergency control, bridge. Readiness confirmed. As usual, Commander, let's hope your services will not be needed."

The bridge front view display was already being relayed to a view screen on Bill's right. Smaller consoles mimicked the views from the other stations on the bridge. Bill could see and anticipate every move being made on the bridge with just a quick glance. For someone wanting to become a captain, this was the best place to learn. If you could anticipate every bridge move using these monitors, you were thinking like the captain. Bill found that he could anticipate nearly every move the captain would make when entering or leaving a system. This would be the first time he would be experiencing the captain's reactions to a mission outside their normal routine.

The navigation screen was displaying the warp exit countdown. Bill watched as it reached zero and felt the slight pull as the computer adjusted to the added forces caused by the sudden loss of warp speed. Behind him, he could hear the reduction in propulsion output as the warp drives shut down. One of the specialists reported, "Privateer's return to sub-light complete. Status board is green. Braking thrusters fired. Deflector power is being equalized from full forward to all emitters."

Bill glanced at the relayed forward view and was impressed by the sight. He was also a little shocked to see a planet directly in front of them. Although it was a still a ways off, at warp speed it had only been a heartbeat away. Good thing we came out of warp when we did, he thought. Several other planets were visible, too. Two were closer together than he would have thought possible. They must be playing havoc on each other in the force of their pulls, he concluded. One of the planets appeared to be taking the worst of it as it was layered in dust particles that provided a wide variety of colors. The other planet contained various layers of dark textures that, from this distance, gave the impression of dark storm clouds. The right side of the screen was partially blocked by a third planet. This third planet appeared larger than the other two combined. The view was panning slowly to the right. This planet blocked any other view in that direction. The view angle paused for a short period before panning back to the front again, then off to the left, finally to come to rest viewing forward once more. Bill continued to take in the sights of this new system, mentally recording everything in detail.

"Braking completed. The ship is running on standard propulsion. Course deviation is thirty-five degrees to port.

Course steadying up on one, two, five degrees. Bridge has completed scanning of the area. Scanning is reporting a small, metallic object thirty degrees to starboard and holding a steady position at 4,188 kilometers left of the foremost planet. The object is just reading on the scanners, but is too far to make out. It is possible that this could be the lost probe," reported the specialist.

Bill could feel the shutdown of the propulsion system before the specialist reported it. Having been on the ship as long as he'd been, any sudden change in sound or vibration would not go without notice. He suspected that the captain wanted to drift in to allow time to check everything out. He knew that she would be cautious out here. Even though the Privateer and her crew were no strangers to isolated places, they usually had some kind of forewarning of what to expect. This time, they were coming in blind without any help from a flight plan. He was sure that the sight of a planet directly in their path did not sit well with her either.

The Privateer drifted along for another thirty-seven minutes before they were close enough for the sensors to clarify the metal object. The Privateer contained a very sensitive set of sensor arrays. This allowed information to be pulled in from a long ways off.

He listened as the specialist started talking again. "Scanning has determined that the metallic object is not the probe. The object is showing small energy output. Scanning is also picking up a large disruption field eleven degrees port of our current heading. A three hundred sixty degree scan has not picked up any other objects. Standard propulsion has resumed."

The Privateer continued deeper into the system for another fifteen minutes. Bill had become interested in the disruption field that was being picked up by one of the sensor arrays. The design of the field was unique.

A strong vibration was felt throughout the compartment. The coffee cups on the consoles began to rattle as each made their own unique sound. Bill grabbed his cup to prevent it from vibrating onto the decking. It was obvious to Bill that the Privateer was braking hard. Looking over at the ship's status display, he could see that all forward thrusters were in use. The nose of the ship began to drift to the right, causing the ship to slip sideways slightly. This was a sign of the thrusters being out of calibration. Another sign of ship fatigue, he thought.

"Standard propulsion has stopped; forward braking thrusters have been activated. Computer auto-guidance has kicked in," reported the specialist, confirming what Bill had already detected.

The continued vibration was affecting the scanners. The information coming in was now choppy and unreliable. Slowly, the ship began to come to a stop, and the vibration began to subside. The ship was now drifting at a pace that was almost too slow to track. The sensors were again supplying useful information. The scanning software was not able to identify the metal composite or identify the energy readings from the metallic object. Next to each composite identifier were the words 'Insufficient Data'.

A small ion pool was catching Bill's attention as he continued to focus on the disruption field. It was five fields, actually. Four of the fields were round pools of small particles that intersected with a larger field in the center. He had never seen anything like this before. He could not imagine what could have caused a pattern like what he was seeing here. The particles gave a hint of some kind of explosion. Bill's thoughts were interrupted when one of the specialists relayed the order, "Commander, you are being requested to report to the bridge."

Bill switched the override controls back to inactive. He ejected and removed the control disc just before leaving the compartment. Taking the nearest turbo lift, he was soon on the bridge again. He could see Sharon and Linda sitting in the command chairs looking at the sensor information that was being displayed on the forward view screen.

Looking up at Bill, Sharon said, "Commander, good to have you back. The captain would like to have a few words with you."

Linda looked up when Sharon finished talking to Bill. Nodding, she said, "Mr. Launtra we are at a loss to explain what we are looking at here." She pointed to the view screen as she continued, "I am hoping that your military background may prove useful in helping us figure this out. Do you have any idea what could cause a disruption field like that?"

Bill looked away from Linda's questioning brown eyes to focus on the sensor-fed viewer. The computer was estimating the total mass of all the particle fields to be well over seven hundred meters in diameter. It reminded Bill of the child's toy, a collide-a-scope if his memory served him right. The small particles were very intense in the center of the four circles and lessened as each of the circles enlarged. One of the things he noticed right away was that a small ion trail that led up to the center of the larger circles. He also noticed that the middle particle field seemed to merge with the other four, almost like an implosion was followed by an explosion…drawing mass inwards and then blowing it out again.

When Bill was an ensign aboard a frigate, they had stumbled upon a destroyed freighter. The freighter had exploded and left a mass of ion larger than the frigate itself. All around and in that ion mass were pieces of the freighter, but its ion mass was not uniform like these particle pools. That mass had been like a large cloud with a strong wind blowing part of it in one direction. Bill wondered if adding the second sensor array would add more detailed information.

"Captain, if I may, I would like to see if having the other sensor brought into play here might add more detail. We may be able to get a better picture of what is within those pools with both arrays working in unison."

On Linda's orders, the second sensor array, currently sweeping in a three hundred sixty degree pattern, was swung around to point at the particle fields. Once in place, the data coming in from it was merged with the data from the other array. The resulting images sharpened up to provide more detail than before.

The sensor computer began to display characters referencing different types of composites. Miniscule pieces of matter scattered within and around the pools began to appear. The sensors were picking up radiated particles of plastic and metal, along with alloys it could not identify. The metal and plastic pieces it could identify were consistent with the materials contained within the Privateer, which were also used to build probes. Bill thought it was a good bet that what was left of the probe was contained within that mass. The question remained as to what the rest of the particles were from. Also puzzling to him was the unique pattern of the pools. He was guessing that a secondary explosion caused the effects of the center particle field. His bet was that the probe's destruction was caused by that explosion. The sensor data was showing a match of ion signatures consistent with the propulsion output of a probe. The rounded pools were still a mystery.

Bill wondered if the probe had collided with another object. Since the probe was so small, the damage it could inflict would seem minimal to something large enough to leave particle fields that wide. But, then again, the particles left behind did not reflect much mass. If it had collided with another object, where was the rest of it, he wondered.

"Captain, my best guess is that the probe struck something that exploded around it. As you can see here," pointing along the viewer, "this ion trail leads right up to the center of the field. The signature of this ion trail is common among our probes and ships, according to the computer analysis. Also, some of the particles in the center of this large field are common with that of the probe, while the particles on the furthest outside field areas are foreign. The computer can not identify the source of material that resides in these particles. It is very confusing because it is a massive explosion but very little debris exists.

"The circular pools of particles are a mystery as well. It looks like four separate explosions. But, from what, I can't even venture a guess. Also, the distance between each field is uniformly spaced, like they were at a calculated distance from each other. I am having a hard time believing that this kind of spacing was accidental. What this all means, I haven't a clue."

"Do you have anything to add, Commander?" Linda asked Sharon.

"Sorry, Captain, but this goes beyond my area of expertise. I agree with Bill that the probe was destroyed here, from what I can't even guess. I recommend we take some additional readings for analysis by the company when we return, and then head for home."

Moving closer to the strange patterns displayed on the screen, Linda said, "Whatever the cause, we are not going to learn much more by staying here. I am interested in what that other object is out there. I don't think it will do any harm to go over and take a look at it. Any objections?"

Both Bill and Sharon said, "No," in unison. Sharon had a disappointed look that gave Linda much pleasure. Yes, Sharon, this entire ordeal was set up just to ruin your plans, she mused.

"Mr. Launtra, I would like you to return to emergency control. Until I get a better feel for what to expect out here, I will feel better with you in there." Linda looked over at Sharon and continued, "Put us on a slow approach to the object. Have the sensor information on the pools recorded for future reference."

Nodding, Sharon began to issue commands to carry out Linda's wishes. Silently she fumed over why they had to approach slowly. In fact, she didn't see why they had to look it over at all. The company executives could always ask the military to come out and take a look if they were interested. They were far better equipped to handle any problems that came up. After all, what was the military for anyway? They were getting lazy these days sitting around waiting for a vessel to get in trouble so they could race to its rescue. It sure didn't look like that object was going anywhere, anytime soon. She decided she would discuss this with the captain when things settled down.

chapter five

The ship had stopped. V'sdntil had watched it break hard and then come to a stop. It was drifting slightly now. The ship was almost directly on top of the intersecting track the other object had traveled. He was sure that they had been able to detect where the other object had been destroyed. This only confirmed his estimation of their technology. He could not detect anything using the buoy's sensor. He was relying on his tracking data to show where the object had been. He had been observing them for some time now. They were just drifting along painstakingly slow. The ship was still too far away to get any detailed information from the probe's sensor. It was closer now, but still too far away to see clearly.

The overlord paced about the bridge. Each step pounding heavily on the metal decking. His long claws clicking the deck with each step. He glanced at the forward view display from time to time. Brk'erst was standing on the opposite side of the bridge to stay out of his way. After what seemed like an eternity to v'sdntil, the other ship started a slow, forward progress again. As synska byf paced, he continued to weigh his options. He had come to a decision that if the vessel had not moved when he returned to his chair, he would break off contact to send a quick message, to the Counsel.

Brk'erst noticed the tracking overling glancing at the overlord. He looked up at the viewer and could see the ship was on the move again. Since synska byf hadn't noticed yet the underlord said, "Overlord, the ship is coming further in system again."

Synska byf turned to look at the viewer. The ship was making a slow, steady approach to the buoy. Much like he would do in this situation, synska byf thought. As the ship neared the buoy, he knew he would have to move to avoid detection. It then occurred to him that if the ship was on the move again, then it was a good bet that it had not stopped to wait for more ships. So what had it stopped for? To sweep the area perhaps.

After what seemed like an eternity, the ship began to take form. The design of the ship and the painted markings intrigued them. They couldn't make any sense of the painted symbols on its bow.

They had a front view of the ship. It was oval-shaped. A round bubble protruded from the top with two round barrels within it, both pointed forward. The strange markings ran in an arc across the bow. Under the bow, two rounded sections, each with a white disk, could be seen. One was stationary and angled forward; the other pointed downward and rotated.

The secondary viewer displayed a two-dimensional view of the ship. Synska byf used a laser pointer to highlight the turret on top. He asked, "What do you make of this top protrusion here?"

The ship was close enough that they could see a slight separation between the cylinder and the ship's hull. Synska byf noted that the computer image showed the barrels barely extended out of the bubbled section.

"See the separation between this section and the rest of the ship?" Synska byf was pointing the light where the cylinder met the ship's hull. He continued, "With that much room between the two, I suspect that this thing rotates. These round objects within it are massive. They appear larger than our launch tubes. What could they launch out of it and how can they even load it? It does not appear to be large enough to load from behind."

"Possibly from underneath in some way. The ship is stopping again. If they attempt to destroy the buoy, we will learn what type of weapon it is." Brk'erst watched synska byf sit in the command chair before he continued. "See these two round sections here?" He pointed to the underside of the ship with his own pointer. "They look like large sensors. I am not sure why they need two of them though."

The overlord started thrumming his claws on the top of the armrest. He said, "It would be nice to see what kind of fire power that ship has, even if it means losing the buoy. If more of these ships come into this system, the Council will be very interested in what they are up against. If they destroy the buoy, we will have to reposition ourselves. That will be the most opportune time to swing around this planet and contact the Council for further instructions," he commented.

Brk'erst started thinking about how they could contact the Council without having to lose contact with this ship. An idea starting forming in his mind to finally hatch into a plan. He said, "Overlord, I have an idea that may allow us to establish communication with the Council without having to leave our position."

"Continue, underlord," synska byf replied curiously.

"If we launch a buoy out a rear tube, we may be able to guide it to a point beyond the planet where it can send and receive signals between our ship and the Council. We could even patch in the images being returned from one buoy and forward to the Council through the other."

After a few beats, synska byf replied, "I have never heard of anyone launching a buoy through a tube before. The buoys are built to withstand the forces of igniting the main booster engine, so we know it can take some abuse.

I think this is worth a try. Work with the tracking overling to make this happen. Let me know when you are ready to launch."

Brk'erst walked over the v'sdntil and asked, "Do you believe that we can connect with the buoy once it is positioned out there?"

V'sdntil started running the commands needed through his head trying to determine how the computer would interpret and execute the commands. He couldn't see why it wouldn't work.

"I'll need to instruct the command control module to not reactivate the main systems until thirty beats after the vacuum switch activates the main computer. I will need to have these commands entered before we launch so I can send them in proper sequence. I would then only need to add the navigational elements to the commands as they are calculated. Should I get started on the command sequences, Underlord?"

"Yes." Turning to the overlord, the underlord said, "Overlord, with your permission, I will oversee the loading of the buoy".

Synska byf nodded his approval. He continued to monitor the other ship. Using the claw of his third finger, he tapped softly on one of his sharp fangs. The two top fangs protruded nearly eight centimeters beyond the upper lip. His bottom two fangs were smaller and only protruded four centimeters beyond his lower lip. The lips had a slight upturn at the fang outlets to allow each tooth to extend outside the lip covering when the mouth was closed. The lips were tan on the outside and streaked yellow and red on the inside. The fangs started out yellow at the gum line and become whiter as they neared the tip. The krracts sharp claws and long teeth, along with their physical build, were all part of their maturity status.

The overlord continued to stare at the other ship. He wondered how long they would be content with looking over the buoy before moving on. It was hard to anticipate what their next move would be. He was hoping they would sit right where they were for a while.

Brk'erst stepped into the center loading bay followed by two overlings and ordered the deck hatch opened. As the hatch opened, it revealed several buoys securely fastened to the decking. They released one and began getting it ready for programming and launch while keeping in contact with the bridge to link the buoy with the computer.

While the work on the buoy was being performed, another overling was directing the connection of the rails that would lead the buoy to the aft launch bay. The buoy was lifted off the deck with a hoist to begin the trek aft. Brk'erst inspected the buoy to insure that no protrusion would strike a roller when the buoy was inserted into one of the tubes. Now loaded into a tube, a large magnetic disc was attached to the back of the buoy. The tube door was then closed. He now decided that the rest was in the hands of the creator.

Captain Eccles looked out at the small metal object as they slowly approached it. When she felt they were close enough, she ordered the Privateer stopped. Using a sensor array and the forward viewer, they gave it a close inspection. Sharon was looking over the data the sensors were pulling in with a tracking specialist. The energy readings, metal composite, and design were all foreign to the computer. The computer showed a high probability that the metal composite of this object was of the same composite as those within the disruption field. She reported these findings to Linda.

Linda noted that the object was not in an orbit of the planet, but stationary. It seemed apparent to her that it was placed here to keep watch on this sector in space. For this reason, she assumed it must be a marker of some kind. Linda heard Sharon move next to her. Linda asked, "Well, Commander, any ideas?"

Sharon looked at her and answered, "It could be an observation device of some kind. It is possible that this thing is recording everything about us. Since we are not picking up any transmitted signals from it, someone would have to come by every now and then to pull the data from it. It looks like it has some kind of receiving antenna on it. That front disk on it is most likely a sensor of some kind."

"It could also be a marker for incoming ships could it not?" Linda countered. She continued without waiting for a reply. "It could be used by incoming ships to request jump coordinates to other points unknown, similar to how we used to use jump markers when early warp engines were not too reliable. These markers could be located and used to help recalculate jump points when a ship had to drop out of warp early. What do you suppose would happen if a ship, which had stopped here to recalculate its jump coordinates, was to enter warp directly into the entry point of the probe? Do you think the probe could have had enough force behind it to penetrate and damage an exiting ship? Sounds kind of farfetched doesn't it?"

Sharon gave this some thought before answering, "I don't know. The timing needed for something like that to have happened makes it seem pretty slim. You would also have to wonder where the rest of the ship is. The probe is too small to blow a ship completely apart. I suppose someone could have come by and hauled it back for repairs. As for a marker, I don't know. It seems to be located in a funny place for that. It seems kind of out of the way to act as a beacon. There is too much planet interference here that could affect your ability to communicate with it. For example, had we come in another few degrees further right, we would not have seen or been able to communicate with this marker. It seems to me that placing the marker closer to where we dropped out would provide better communication options with the thing."

For the first time, Linda was actually impressed with Sharon. Perhaps there was something working inside that head of hers after all, she thought. "You may be right Sharon. If we take your theory that it could be an observation device, could it have transmitted our presence already? Perhaps, before we could have detected it. If so, we could expect some company soon," Linda pondered.

Ensign Marcy Hawk was sitting at the communications console eavesdropping on the captain and the exec. Marcella's fiery red hair made the slim black communication headpiece she was wearing stand out. She was short and stocky with a light complexion. She was well liked because of her mild, easygoing mannerism. She had relieved the specialist on duty as an excuse to be on the bridge. It was where the action was, as she saw it. While listening to the bridge conversation, she was playing with the various slide controls that filtered frequencies in and out. She liked the sounds that came through as her fingers worked the various controls. It was almost like playing a tune. Only half listening, something caught her attention. She looked at her fingers to see where the slides were in their settings. She began to adjust the controls to narrow in on that one particular sound. After a few minutes, she was able to isolate it. It came in waves that were constant, but not repetitive, at least that she could tell. To her, they appeared to be generated signals as opposed to random space chatter. She switched over control to the ship's computer to see if it could determine a pattern or maybe even identify the signal source. She didn't get any recognition hits from the computer. She wondered if she had intercepted a communication band of some kind.

While she let the computer continue to digest the signal, she decided to work on determining where the signal was being picked up in relation to her position. To do this, she activated the antenna directional display screen that showed a computer-generated image of the antenna array. She entered in the megahertz that matched the signal she had intercepted. Colored waves disappeared, leaving just the single strand. It was easy to tell from which direction the signal was hitting the receiver. Nearly a third of the circle was being hit by it. The wave appeared to be coming from one of the planets. Marcy continued to monitor the display, watching closely as the planet slowly rotated. The rotation of the planet did not alter the direction of the signal. This was a strong indication that the signal was not being transmitted from the planet's surface. But, the sensor had not shown any satellites or relay stations orbiting there either. That left only one conclusion: it had to be bouncing off the planet or its atmosphere. This was the limit of what she would be able to get from the communication software.

Feeding the communication data into the tracking computer, she switched over to the tracking computer remote feed. She pulled up the system view from the tracking display. She then added in the data from the communication feed. She requested a feedback track on the signal. She was instantly rewarded with the signal track from source to receiver. The tracking computer was showing the source to be the object in front of them with a signal track towards the planet. The tracking computer showed the left side of the wide signal arc striking and bouncing off the planet almost directly into the ship's path.

She swung her chair around and said, "Captain, I am picking up a signal that appears to be generating from the object. It is being directed towards the planet tracking has marked as P-3. We are picking up the bounce back from it. I fed this through the translation logic, but it didn't find a match. I doubt if we are getting more than a small portion of what is actually being transmitted. The sending beam is tight, so we are only getting what is deflecting back."

Linda said to Sharon, "It appears that your guess of a monitoring device was a good one."

"So it seems. It would be a good bet that someone knows we are here, too," Sharon responded.

Staring back out at the object, Linda said, "That would explain the location. From here this device can pick up incoming ships before a ship will be able to detect the object. I don't like not knowing who owns this device and what they are monitoring this area for. I have to assume that this device picked up the probe and whatever came along to check it out, destroyed it. They probably aren't going to be any happier with us here either. I think it is time for us to get the hell out of here."

"You have my vote on that one and the sooner the better. This place is giving me the creeps all of a sudden," Sharon responded.

"It may already be too late. The probes are pretty efficient at collecting data and moving on. They don't linger in one area too long. We know from the ion track that the probe was heading out of the system when something destroyed it. What we don't know is what direction it came in from. Apparently close enough to target and destroy the probe. Plot us a course to take us to a jump point closer to where we entered from. Stay clear of the path that the probe had taken. Let's get this tub moving," Linda ordered.

❖ ❖ ❖

By the time brk'erst had returned to the bridge, synska byf was pacing again. He stopped when he notice brk'erst. Tilting his head, he jerked it slightly toward the forward monitor. "No change. If nothing else, at least they do not seem to be in any hurry. Is the buoy ready to be launched, underlord?"

"Almost, Overlord. The buoy has been loaded into aft tube number two," replied brk'erst as he walked over to the tracking station. V'sdntil was busy entering the last of the commands he anticipated would be needed to control the buoy. Brk'erst continued, "It looks like we are just about ready now."

"Very good, underlord. You may launch as soon as you are ready," synska byf said as he resumed his pacing.

Brk'erst reviewed the command sequences v'sdntil had entered. Satisfied with the sequence he had him lock them in. He knew that some of the commands would have to be entered on the fly based on what happened as the buoy moved along its projected course. But that couldn't be helped. Brk'erst biggest concern was the magnetic disked used to launch objects from the tubes. While the mines had shielded circuitry, the buoys did not. He could only hope that the circuits were far enough away from the buoy's outer surfaces to survive the magnetic buildup that would occur in the tube.

He walked back over to synska byf and said, "We are ready to launch. It will all depend on how sturdy the buoy is and if the circuitry can handle the magnetic charge. With your permission, Overlord, I would like to rotate the ship to place the aft tube at the proper angle."

"See to it, underlord," synska byf responded.

chapter SIX

In the aft launch bay, the launch light illuminated on the display board for tube two. Inside the tube, an electromagnetic ring powered up, which drew the buoy towards the tube hatch. The disc, placed on the buoy when it was loaded, attached solidly against the hatch's inner frame. The disc now blocked five pressure outlets in the tube hatch. Steam was forced through the tubes that ended at the five blocked holes. As the pressure increased so did the power to the electromagnetic ring. When the steam had reached the calculated pressure, the electromagnetic ring shut off. The five holes released their built up pressure against the disc with a loud bang.

No one on the bridge said a word as the buoy shot out the tube. The buoy was a blur as it headed away from the rear of the ship. A pressure switch on the buoy activated the main power unit, and the buoy came on line. The main propulsion motors fired per the first command sequence. The blast from the boosters blew the magnetic disk off of the buoy.

On the bridge's rear display screen, v'sdntil watched the plume of vapors left behind as the propulsion units fired. He calculate how long before the braking sequence needed to begin. The buoy's computer would keep it on its current course until directed otherwise. He fed the current position, the time of that positional fix, and the rate of speed the buoy was traveling into the computer and then pinpointed the exact location of where the buoy was to be stopped.

V'sdntil constantly monitored the buoy's progress on the tracking display. As the buoy neared the brake point he prepared to send the next sequence command. He sent out the signal and included a fuel status request.

The buoy rotated around so it was now facing towards the ship. V'sdntil was not happy to see that the fuel burn rate was higher than he had anticipated. He now estimated that once the buoy was stopped there would be very little left to position the buoy, or keep it from drifting. He sent the sequence to begin the braking

"Underlord, the buoy's fuel burn rate is higher than expected. I should be able to bring the buoy to the right location but I am not sure I will be able to keep it there for long," v'sdntil reported.

Before brk'esrt could respond, a warning tone went off indicating a problem with the buoy. He walked over to v'sdntil to see what was happening.

"Sorry Underlord, one of the buoy's thrusters has misfired. It is pushing the buoy off course slightly. With the loss of the extra thrust the buoy will end up further out than I had planned," v'sdntil said

"Recalculate the braking distance overling and determine if this is going to create a problem with trying to communicate with it," the underlord responded.

"The buoy will stop approximately nineteen hundred fnifs beyond the intended location, Underlord," v,sdntil answered. "It should still be in a position to sequence between us and the Council."

As the buoy came to a stop the overlord sent the final command to extend and activate the antenna. It wasn't long before v'sdntil had the communication link established.

"The link is completed and ready for your use Underlord," v'sdntil said. He was relieved that this was over.

"Overling, you have done well. You will be mentioned in my report," synska byf said. He then said to the underlord, "I will be in my living space preparing a message for the Council. Let me know if anything changes."

V'sdntil was stunned by the comment from the overlord. To be recognized by him was a rare occurrence. His worms were going to taste even better at the end of this work cycle.

Bill Launtra continued his wait in the emergency control room as ordered. They had been under way again for about three hours. He would have loved to be on the bridge right now and hear what was going on. The probe had been destroyed. That was a given. The sensor arrays were searching the smaller planet for energy readings. Since this object appeared to be signaling in that direction, he suspected the captain wanted to be sure that they had not missed anything.

Linda was part of a small group that huddled around the images returned by the sensor arrays. Her back was sore from leaning over for so long. She straightened up and tried to work the kinks out of her spine. They had not detected any sign of power usage anywhere on the planet so far. The Privateer did not carry any probes, so they could not send one out to see what was around the other side of the planet.

Linda shook her head and decided she has spent enough time looking for ghost. She headed for the captain's office, which was a small compartment just off the bridge. As she was heading for the door, she called back over her shoulder, "The Bridge is yours, Commander".

Once inside her small office, Linda sat at her desk and opened up a communication recording. She took a few moments to collect her thoughts before activating the recorder.

She began:

ATD: 1670; Date: 2246; Priority AAAA; From: Captain Linda Eccles; Privateer; To: CEO Ernest T. Leander; ADM Wilson Swensen; Message as follows:

I have reached the destination of the last known position of the probe 13-115-98. Based on evidence at this location, determined probe to be destroyed by unknown source. Highly suspect probe was destroyed with hostile intent. Probe and contents lost. Found small object believed to be a monitoring device close by. On further inspection, found object to be transmitting messages to unknown location. Subject unknown. Language unknown. Have reason to believe that our presence has been detected. Expected action to be taken by receivers of signal is unknown. Requesting permission to return to station. Will stand by at jump point 478.76459.110 to await further orders. Respectfully, Linda Eccles, Captain, Privateer;

Linda played back the cryptic message. Satisfied with the wording, she notified the communication specialist to have it transmitted immediately. She also asked to have a copy of her transmission added to the ship's log. She then started pacing the office, rerunning the prior events through her mind, looking for anything she may have missed.

After take a seat again, she notified the communication specialist to open a comm channel throughout the ship. Once it was ready she said, "This is the Captain. After searching the area we have determined that the probe has been destroyed. It is unknown for sure what caused its destruction. We are now heading back to the jump point to head for home."

❖ ❖ ❖

Overlord synska byf was pacing his living space again while waiting for a return message from the Council. By his calculation, it should be coming in any beat now. He had informed them of what had transpired so far. He also informed them that his communication setup was only temporary due to the limited time with the buoy. He asked for their recommendation on how to proceed. It had all come down to a waiting game now. What would the ship do? What would the Council want him to do? Would they send help in dealing with this ship? What would he do if they told him to handle it himself? He had never faced a situation like this before. There were too many unknowns to his liking. This ship could pose a much larger tactical problem should they order him to detain it. He knew nothing about their capability or how it compared to that of the probe. Would he take the blame if it got away? The questions and problems continued to pile up in his mind.

The tone signaling the incoming message brought him out of his thoughts. Walking over, he selected the options that allowed him to review it. After a few beats, he headed out of his living space. He had his orders and help was on its way.

The members at the Council were at a loss for what to do next. They had received the message from the overlord of the bfnor torrnt requesting help in dealing with an alien ship. They had a fleet of war ships docked without any crews. Most of the overlords and underlords had moved on to other positions and the overlings had scattered across krractssnk. Underlings were no problem, as they could always round them up from just about anywhere.

The Council members had their supporting overlings begin a listing of all overlords who had previously commanded the docked ships, then a list of serving underlords. From this, they were able to find four overlords and five underlords to fill the needs of commanding the ships. They were quickly summoned to the Council chamber. Overlings were also selected from those that had space flight experience and were close enough to be rounded up in a hurry. From the main labor pool, all the underlings waiting for work assignments were gathered up and sent to five ships. The ships selected were those that could be serviced and sent out quickly. Even before the summoned overlords had gathered, underlings were already loading supplies onto the ships.

There was one final task to be completed. Who would lead the fleet? Each of the overlords were briefed about the mission and assigned a ship. The Council members now sat down to discuss the options for the overall commander. After nearly five ten-beats, a decision had been reached. They all agreed that jeftrk byf was the krracts best suited to this task. He had prior experience commanding a cruiser. Although he was not the best choice overall, he was considered the best choice among those closest to get the fleet moving. The call went out for him to come to the Council chamber. The Council members waited for his arrival.

Jeftrk byf was sitting at his command station two buildings down from the Council command center. He was reviewing the latest reports on the status of all the mines currently deployed. He still had the buoy status sheet to review as well. His mind kept drifting away as he wondered why the Council had pulled the bfnor torrnt away from its current assignment. He had not been told why they needed the ship, only that the Council was reassigning it until further notice. The bfnor torrnt was supposed to be on its way home to be reloaded and redeployed into another sector. This delay was going to make him have to delay the return of another minelayer. It was hard enough to get krracts to work on these ships as it was, he thought.

Shaking his head, jeftrk byf tried again to return his attention to the status sheets. He was annoyed when an overling came in and broke his concentration again. He questioned sharply, "Yes, overling, what is it?"

The overling responded, "Sorry for the interruption, Overlord. You are requested to report to the Council chamber at once." With that, the overling bowed slightly, and then backed out of the room.

Jeftrk byf again shook his head. Just what he needed! More confusion. The only time anyone was called to the Council chamber was when the Council was upset about something. He wondered what they could be upset about. He was not behind schedule, yet, at least that they would know about. He wondered if this had something to do with his minelayer they had confiscated. That must be it, he thought. If they damaged the ship somehow, he was going to request they release a destroyer to him until another one could be built to replace it. All the minelayers he had could barely keep up with the demand. This was all he needed was to be down a ship. He stood up and proceeded out of the building to take the short walk to the Council building. As he walked along he started wondering if the overlord on that minelayer has screwed up. Since he recommended that overlord, it would not reflect well on his judgment.

The front of the Council building had always impressed him. He walked up the fifteen steps to enter the front landing covered by a rounded archway. Four massive pillars held up the front awning. Each pillar was etched with different hunting scenes involving past Council members. The one that always fascinated him was the scene of the first Council head taking down two large bafplt. Even though jeftrk byf was a good-sized krracts, he would have been hard pressed to take down even a single bafplt, considering the size of them in the scene. He wondered who had decided on that etching. Most likely, the sli himself those many solar cycles ago, he figured. He shook his head as he entered the building.

Once he was through the archway and into the main entry hall, jeftrk byf walked to the stairway that led to the second floor. He could see that the two large stone doors leading to the Council chamber were open. He could also see the long table in the middle with Council members sitting behind it. He entered the chamber and walked up to the single chair placed in the middle of the room. He waited patiently to be addressed. Some of the members were holding private conversations with each other.

After a few beats, the Council leader sitting in the center of the group tapped the tabletop with the claws of his right hand. The sound echoed loudly in the chamber, bringing a halt to the multitude of side conversations. The Council members looked directly at jeftrk byf as the Council leader said, "Overlord, be seated. A situation is developing in the rhepp system that needs immediate attention. At this very moment, we have five ships being prepared. Each ship is already crewed and will most likely be supplied by the time you arrive. You are to take command of this fleet and head out to the rhepp system with all haste. Once there, you will take charge of the situation. We have been receiving messages from the bfnor torrnt that a ship has entered that system in response to some kind of tracking device they had destroyed. We have ordered the overlord of the bfnor torrnt to monitor the situation until you arrive. You are to disable that ship and tow it back here for the Council to inspect. Although we would prefer not to harm the crew, disabling that ship is your first priority. Any questions?"

Jeftrk byf was caught by surprised. He wasn't sure what to say at the moment. He wondered why they had selected him to lead this venture. He also wondered what this other ship meant. Was it ahead of a larger force yet to arrive? Could this be a wandering vessel similar to his minelayers that had stumbled into the rhepp system? Well, no matter; he could handle the situation. He finally said, "Do we know the capabilities of this ship, such as its armament?"

"The information from Overlord synska byf has kept us updated on the ship's progress, but he has not been able to provide much in the way of details as of yet. One thing we do know is that the tracking device they destroyed appeared to have advanced shielding. The Overlord feels that this vessel is connected to the device and most likely has the same capabilities. All the information we have reviewed will be made available to you on board the ship."

"What ships are being prepared?"

"You will have the cruisers ghontuf and piirfh njyfn with the tuilmf, njyfur lguunc, and kaffnur dneui for support. The ghontuf and piirfh njyfn are paired ships, so you can choose which one you want to command from. We have assigned an Overlord to four of the ships already. You can shift commands of these assignments as you feel necessary."

Jeftrk byf thought some more on this. He was thrilled with the chance to prove his abilities to the Council, but he was also concerned with the lack of information available to him. He was sure that he would have a very short time to get caught up to date and make the right decisions. But, still, he would have a five-to-one superiority plus the bfnor torrnt, even though he was not sure the minelayer would be much help in this situation.

The Council leader took the silence to mean he did not have any more questions. He said, "Overlord, time is short.

The sooner you get to your ship, the faster your fleet can move out. The bfnor torrnt awaits your arrival."

Linda was sitting behind her desk in her cabin with she was interrupted by the comm unit buzzing. She activated it and said, "Yes?"

"Captain, a message is being received marked for your eyes only," Sharon reported.

"Very well. Have it routed to me in here and join me Commander." She then watched as the transmission was relayed and loaded onto her terminal. As Sharon entered the office, Linda pointed her to a chair. She then turned the monitor so they both could see it. Replying yes, she was rewarded with picture images of both the admiral and the CEO. They were staring directly at the screen. As the CEO spoke, the image changed to a close-up of his face only.

"Captain, we were surprised to hear that the probe had been destroyed and that you may find yourself in a compromising situation. Both Admiral Swensen and I agree that it is not in your best interest to remain on station there. The admiral here is taking steps to address your findings and will take over in that area. Upon receiving this message, you are to hightail it out of there and return here for debriefing." Turning to the admiral, he asked if he had anything to add. The image changed to the admiral's face as he started to speak.

"Captain, we will be sending a scouting vessel with backup support to your location to continue this investigation. If anything should become known to you, prior to your departure, that you feel would be of use to us, please relay it without delay. Our forces will be on their way before your ship returns here." With that, the admiral nodded to the CEO.

"Your return jump vector had been given top priority. All shipping lanes will be kept open until you arrive. That is all, Captain. We hope to see you soon and God's speed," The CEO said. The message ended.

"Scouting vessel with support, my ass. What they are really saying is that they are sending in the military," commented Sharon.

"They didn't leave any room for interpretation. Get out of harm's way and let the cavalry come charging to the rescue. But, to be honest, the sooner we get out of here the better I will feel. This whole thing has my hair standing on end. The longer we stay here, the better the chances we are going to end up having to answer to someone." Linda ran her hands through her hair as she continued, "The sooner we reach the jump point the happier I will be. If nothing else, at least we have a free ticket to jump home without having to wait for an arrival time and vector. Go ahead and return to the bridge. I will be there shortly"

"Do you want me to increase speed to hurry us along," Sharon asked.

Linda gave this some thought before replying, "No, we better not. If the CEO sends us another message, we will not get it."

"Very well, Captain," Sharon responded as she headed off.

Linda could tell that Sharon was disappointed with her response. Screw her, she thought. Linda returned to the daily reports, insuring no problems had been reported that she should be aware of before making a jump for home.

"Commander, I have the bridge." Linda said as she entered the bridge and took her seat.

Sharon, already sitting in the other chair, replied loudly, "The captain has the bridge." To the captain directly she said, "Everything is in order. No problems to report."

"Very well, Commander. You are relieved," Linda responded. She ignored Sharon's departure from the bridge. She then opened a channel to Bill and asked, "Bill, this is the captain. You still awake down there?"

Bill had been napping in his chair with his feet on the countertop. He was on his second consecutive shift in emergency control. He nearly fell over when the intercom startled him awake.

"Yes, Captain, I am still alive and kicking here," he quipped.

"Sorry to keep you down there so long, Bill. Once we can jump for home, I will get you some relief," Linda said

"No problem, Captain," Bill responded just before the captain cut off the channel.

After making a trip throughout the ship, synska byf returned to the bridge. He walked over to his command chair and spoke to brk'esrt as he sat down. "I have been ordered by the Council to stay on station here and monitor this ship. If it tries to leave, I am to detain it. The Council is sending more ships to take over the situation, and we will provide assistance once they arrive. Their message did not contain how many ships or who the overlords would be. With any luck, this ship will just stay put until they arrive."

"Any idea how we are to detain them if they decide to leave?" asked brk'erst.

"Not at the moment, underlord. Let's just hope that we don't have to figure that one out," synska byf responded.

Brk'erst nodded and turned to make his rounds to each of the bridge stations to insure that all the overlings were keeping busy. He was standing at the tracking station when the other ship began to move. Looking over at synska byf, he could tell the overlord had already noticed the ship turning away from the buoy. The overlord had a very sour look at the moment.

Synska byf stared at the main viewer as the ship continued its turn until it was heading away at a steady pace. While watching it slowly depart, he quickly tried to decide how best to handle this. His orders were specific: prevent the ship from leaving. He thought about heading round the opposite side of the planet in the hope of cutting them off. But, he knew that unless the ship continued to maintain its slow pace, they had little chance of outpacing it with the time it would take to get around the planet. He came to the conclusion that there was only one real choice for him to make. He needed to give them another reason to stay.

"Ahead, half speed. Keep your course steady so we can keep in contact with the communication buoy. As soon as we clear the planet, break contact with the tracking buoy and switch to our own sensor." Synska byf was hoping that the other ship would see them arrive and stop to investigate. His only hope was to keep them around until the other ships could arrive. He hoped they did not take their time getting here. He tuned out the repeated commands of brk'erst as his orders were being carried out. He was trying to think about his next steps just in case the ship failed to stop. He would have to alter course soon to keep from losing too much distance. But, as soon as they turned to pursue, they would quickly lose contact with the communication buoy. He didn't like the idea of being cut off again.

After much consideration, he finally said, "Underlord, have a message sent to the Council stating that the ship has begun to leave and that we are in pursuit. Let them know that we will have to cut communications right after sending the message. Once the message is relayed, alter course to pursue."

"Captain, contact bearing twenty-four degrees off our aft end! Course one, six, three relative, speed is thirty-five thousand meters per minute! It is definitely a ship, but tracking does not have any record of the design!" an excited specialist reported.

"Put it on the main view screen. Have Commander Bresee report to the bridge," ordered Linda. The right half of the main viewer was replaced by an image of the rear view. A ship could be seen just clearing the planet at a right angle to their course. The current magnification was not close enough to allow much of the ship's details to be seen.

"Set magnification to maximum, centering on the vessel," Linda ordered. The image was enlarged with the ship now centered in the display. They were looking at the side of the ship as it moved out from behind the planet. The bottom of the ship was flat, the front section rounded, and the back end flattened out. The side image prevented the viewer from showing much of the rear exhaust ports. The top of the ship had another rounded section that started about a quarter of the way back from the bow and continued on until it met up with a stepped down section about an eighth of the way from the exhaust ports. Linda thought it looked like an old-fashion submarine she had learned of in her history lessons, way back when. It just needed a conning tower on top to complete the picture.

Linda ignored Sharon's arrival on the bridge. Once Sharon had sat down Linda said, "They are too close to that planet to have just jumped in. Familiar with this system or not, no one in their right mind would come into a system that close to a planet. They either came in farther out where they are just now reaching us or they were there the entire time. Considering that signal we were trying to track down, I would bet a month's credit that they were the recipients of it."

"I agree. The timing was just too perfect that this ship would pop out just as we decide to leave. However, if I was commanding that ship, I would have opted to come out on the other side of that planet. This would have put them in a much better position to head us off," Sharon offered.

"We can sit here speculating all day, but it will not help us determine what to do next. But the real question is what we should do about it. They showed their hand by exposing themselves. I can't help but take this as a way to delay us. Get us interested in them so we don't leave. If that is what they intend, I don't plan on playing along." Linda stated testily.

"I would feel much better if we were closer to our jump point should things get a bit dicey," Sharon replied.

Linda added, "True. When we reach the jump point and can kick out of here at any time, I may take some time to look them over more closely. Until then, we keep going. It's their show, so let's see what comes of it, shall we?"

The other ship had completely cleared the planet and was now slowly turning towards the Privateer. It had not increased speed to overtake them. As an afterthought, Linda said to Sharon, "I think it would be a good idea to have Lieutenant Ladd relieve Commander Launtra so he can move into the weapons station. See to it, Commander."

Rebecca was lying on the floorboard of one of the shuttles trying to reach a circuit connection under the dash. She had her right hand snaked in as far as it would go through the maze of wiring, but she was still not able to reach it. She swore to herself as she tried to push her hand in farther. She thought about how much easier this would be if the designers had put access panels in the dash. She sure wasn't going to miss these crafts when they were replaced. She knew the Mark Sevens had access panels, making them much easier to work on. She needed to reach the connection so she could remove the sensor switch for the portside stabilizer, which was giving false readings from time to time.

With her hand just a few millimeters from the connector, she jumped when a specialist stuck his head in and said, "Rebecca, you're wanted on the bridge. Commander Bresee asked that you report right away."

Swearing as she now tried to remove her hand from the multitude of wires, she asked, "What in the world does the exec want with me? I don't remember doing anything that would have gotten her mad at me." She glanced at the status display to see that the ship had not changed course recently. She doubted if they needed a shuttle for anything. As she headed towards the lift she said, "See what you can do with getting that damn sensor replaced. I'll be damned if I can get at it. Cut a hole in the dash if you have to. We are going to junk them anyway when we get back."

Rebecca stepped out of the lift and stopped to review the scene on the bridge. Both the captain and exec were sitting in the command chairs with their backs toward her. She was surprised to see a ship on the viewer. "You wanted to see me, Commander?" Even though she tried to appear calm, her voice gave away her nervousness.

"Stand easy, Rebecca. You have been working with Commander Launtra to be rated for taking up station in emergency control, correct? Do you feel confident with assuming that role now?" Linda asked.

"Yes, Captain, Commander Launtra had been training me pretty hard. I have a clear understanding of all the functions performed there." Rebecca responded, hoping she wasn't overselling herself.

Linda continued, "I would like you to relieve Commander Launtra in emergency control right away. You will remain on station until relieved yourself. Inform the Commander that he is to move into weapons control and report to us his readiness. Any questions, Lieutenant?"

"Not that I can think of. I will inform Commander Launtra that I am relieving him and he is to move into weapons control. I'm on my way." She turned quickly and left the bridge.

As she rode the lift, Rebecca wondered why she was being asked to take over emergency control. She was a backup to Bill, but she never expected to actually take over his responsibilities, as long as he was around anyway. Then it hit her, that this was all being executed because of that ship she saw. Exiting the lift, she proceeded to emergency control and found Bill looking at the image of the unknown ship. There was a lively conversation about the shape of the ship and what purpose it served. She wondered if the captain was worried that this ship would fire on them. She noted that they were still moving at half standard speed, so it didn't appear to be a chase yet. She wondered who they were and what all the fuss was about.

Rebecca suddenly noticed that Bill was looking over at her. "Commander, I have been instructed to relieve you. You are ordered to head to the weapons control station and report in from there."

Bill slid his chair over until he came to the communication relay. He pressed the comm switch and said, "Bridge, this is Commander Launtra. I am being relieved in emergency control by Lieutenant Ladd. I will be proceeding to the weapons control room shortly. I will report in once I arrive."

After a short delay, the communication specialist responded back, "Your message has been relayed, Commander."

Bill waited until the comm light went out before saying, "Very well, Rebecca. Emergency control is yours. If you have to take control, don't run us into a planet, okay?"

"I'll try," she responded with a smile. She then watched Bill as he exited the compartment.

On his way to the weapons compartment, Bill pondered that the captain must be concerned about the intent of the ship trailing them. He was surprised, however, that the captain had Rebecca replace him rather than Sharon. Rebecca had done a good job of learning what Bill had taught her, but she had not been involved in a simulated test of having to take control of the ship. He thought that Sharon would have been a better choice, but suspected that the captain had her reasons.

Bill entered the weapons control room and noticed right away that one of the weapon specialists was tracking the other ship on the targeting computer. The word passive was displayed on the top of each of the small display screens. Bill wasn't concerned as he knew that active tracking could not be initiated until he released the control lock on the targeting computer.

Walking over to the control console, Bill sat down and activated the comm link. "Bridge, Commander Launtra. Weapons station crewed and ready. Tracking is locked into the rear vessel in passive mode."

"Mr. Launtra, this is the captain. You are cleared to unlock the weapons system, but remain in passive mode until further ordered."

"Very well, Captain. Weapons system will be unlocked and kept passive."

"Thank you, Mr. Launtra."

"Take the track off that ship. I don't want the turret swinging their way when I activate the system. Staring down those barrels would scare the pee-water out of me, I suspect it would them also," Bill ordered.

Once the track has been turn off, Bill entered his security code. The weapons station seemed to come alive as buttons lit up and display screens switched to varying modes of images. Bill entered the command to release the tracking controls from its locked mode to ready. All that needed to happen now was for tracking to be switched from passive to active. He could hear the massive capacitors charging up as the noise filtered though from the conduits. Bill then glanced at the turret status display. The turret was facing forward as he had expected. Bill was now ready should the captain decide to use the guns. He then asked a specialist to go out and get some sandwiches and coffee for everyone. He sat in the chair in front of the command console, where he figured he would be until they made the jump to warp. He glanced at the nearest tracking display screen to see what the other ship was doing. He then leaned back in the chair and wondered what was going to happen next. The sudden change in responsibilities seemed to wake him up. He had not slept in a while now, but he knew that the captain and exec must have been as tired as he was.

"Open a channel throughout the ship," Linda ordered, and then continued when the connection was completed, "This is the Captain. A ship has appeared aft of our position. It doesn't show any hostile intent, so I intend to leave it alone. We will continue on our way in the hopes they will just observe our departure. To play it safe, close and lock down all hatches and passageway doors. If damage occurs in your compartment, remember your evacuation drills. First priority is breathing apparatuses, second is the nearest safe compartment exit point, and the third is to close off the damaged compartment upon exiting. Remember to keep your cool and think clearly. Captain out."

Now being tracked with the sensor from his ship, synska byf watched the other ship slowly move away. Brk'erst was standing at his side, ready to react to any order his overlord gave. With this rear view of the fleeing ship, they could now see the two cutout sections near the exhaust ports. Each cutout appeared to have a seam down the middle of where it was cut back into the hull. Synska byf was guessing that these were hatches that allowed entry into that section of the ship. He didn't mention this out loud, but he made a mental note of it. He read the figures below the display of the ship to see if it had changed speed. Nothing had changed since they turned to follow.

Synska byf leaned toward brk'erst saying, "They give no acknowledgement of our presence. I would expect they are able to detect us. I have to take this to mean that they are going to ignore us. How would you handle this situation, underlord?"

"We could increase speed to see if they will do the same. This may help to determine if they intend to flee from us or if they are just ignoring us for now," brk'erst answered.

"I am sorry to interrupt, Underlord, but I am picking up an increased energy reading. It is located sixteen fnifs under the top protrusion," reported the tracking overling.

The main view screen marked the location of the increased energy reading in white. Synska byf and brk'erst looked at the readings that registered below the ship.

"I think we can rule out propulsion as they have not increased speed. It is way too early for them to be charging up for a jump to light speed, unless they are desperate enough to try to jump from their current location. Since we have not really threatened them, that seems unlikely. The only thing really left would be that they are charging weapons," synska byf commented.

"If they are charging their weapon, it is a good indication that they must be feeling threatened," offered brk'erst.

Synska byf replied, "Perhaps, or maybe they are looking for revenge for the object we destroyed, and we are the current target available to them. I think we should them a signal, something simple to see if we can put them at ease. Have the communication overling send out a message stating that we would like to talk with them. Of course, I don't expect them to be able to read it. It may give them pause as to our intent. This might make us look a little friendlier to them. Be prepared to take evasive action, just in case they are looking for revenge."

Bowing slightly to show he understood the request, brk'erst walked over to the communication station to supervise the creation of the message. When it was ready he said, "Be sure to transmit it across all frequencies to insure they get it, overling."

After receiving a confirmation, he returned to the overlord. Once there, he said, "The message is being sent as ordered, Overlord." He watched the screen to see what would happen next.

"Notice that the energy reading has leveled off. This has to be related to their weapons system. Be ready to veer off at max propulsion on my order should they turn on us suddenly." The overlord sat back into his chair and waited. He was suddenly very aware of how venerable his ship was at the moment. He was very impatient for the other ships to arrive and take over this hunt.

chapter SEVEN

Marcy was once again sitting at the communication station. She took over when the other ship had been sighted as an excuse to be on the bridge. She knew that she wasn't fooling the captain or the exec any, but she also knew they wouldn't mind having her on the bridge either, as she was the most experienced of the specialists. Listening to the conversation between the captain and the first officer, she almost missed the sound of the computer switching on the signal recorder. She pressed the headset closer to her ear so she could hear over the conversations on the bridge. The message sounded repetitive and she noticed it was coming in on all frequencies. The signal strength was pegging the top of the scale. There was little doubt in her mind that it was meant to get their attention. She glanced over to insure that the computer was capturing each revolution of the signal.

Once Marcy was sure that the message was repetitive, she switched over to the recorder and played back the captured sounds. The varying tones sounded familiar to her, so she decided to switch over to the earlier recordings she had captured. The two signals had familiar patterns within them. She routed the new signal through the translation module and waited for the results. The computer failed to come up with a match from other known signals. She altered the commands to have the computer try to decipher the message. She was hoping that some of it could be translated.

"Captain, I just recorded a signal I am pretty sure is coming from that ship. They are transmitting a repetitive message on all frequencies. I have the computer trying to translate it now. I am certain it contains the same signal pattern that we recorded bouncing back from the planet."

The captain swung her chair to the right as far as it would go. She had to glance back over her shoulder to see Marcy. "Stay on top of it. Let me know if you can decipher any of it."

She let the chair swing back around to talk with Sharon. "A signal? Are they really trying to communicate with us? We can't do much about a signal we can't translate. I doubt they would expect us to be able to understand it. Why send it then? They are trying to get our attention, I'm sure of it." She paused a moment before continuing. "This has to be a delaying tactic, but why?"

Sharon smiled as she said, "Maybe they're the reception committee trying to ask us over for tea."

Linda looked at Sharon and replied sharply, "You won't be smiling so much if they send a plasma blast up our exhaust port. I don't need to remind you that our aft shielding is not our strongest asset." Linda paused to think things through. She put her thumb and index finger over her chin while slowly massaging her left cheek. She then looked back at Sharon and said, "I think it's best that we don't get distracted from reaching our jump point. I would like to keep some measure of distance between them and us in case I need room to maneuver. I hate this guessing game. Just what the hell are they up to?"

Sharon knew better than to take this situation lightly with the captain. She responded, "I don't know either Captain. But I agree that keeping our distance makes a lot of sense right now."

The counter on the translation computer passed forty-three thousand passes through the recorded message.

It had not been able to pick out a single word. Marcy added in some samplings of the feedback recordings from the other signals, but she still could not get the computer to sort out any of the message. She finally gave up and switched it off. Turning to Linda again, she said, "I'm sorry, Captain, no luck in breaking down the message. The computer is unable to decipher even one word. It was able to validate that the two signals are of a like nature. It is a good bet that both signals were generated from the same language base."

"Very well, Ensign. Thanks for trying," Linda responded without turning towards her. Linda knew that the Privateer was running out of time. She was going to have to decide what to do and hope it was the right decision. The earliest she could expect another ship to arrive from Rapitine was twenty-three days, and that was only if they had left already. She was only told they would be gone before she arrived. She thought it was a good bet that this other ship was much closer to home. The probe had been spotted, tracked, a signal sent, and a ship responded in just a few days. If her theory was correct, she reminded herself. If this ship was responsible for the probe's destruction, she knew it would be unwise to think that other ships weren't already on their way to back this one up. She glanced up at the pursuing ship's image again. No, she knew her best option was to get the hell out of here and let the military handle this one. She decided she wasn't paid enough to get her ass shot off.

Linda left the bridge and headed into her office to send a message. She had told Sharon to inform her the minute something changed. She sent an updated message about the arrival of the ship and the signal they had received. She also noted in the message that she would not wait for a return reply. Returning to the bridge, she glanced at her watch. After several seconds, she ordered, "Standard propulsion, all ahead full."

Sharon relayed, "Navigator, increase speed to full ahead." She could feel the vibration under her feet as the Privateer's massive propulsion system increased power. It never ceased to amaze her how much the propulsion system could be heard and felt throughout a ship, no matter how the ship builders tried to mask it. She glanced at the view screen to watch as they began pulling away from the trailing ship. She read the tracking information below the ship's image to see if any change was recorded in course or speed. So far, the other ship seemed content with laying back. She hoped it stayed that way.

The captain spoke softly to Sharon, "Let's hope they just watch us leave. If they attempt to follow or overtake us, I will give them a 'shot across the bow'. I intend to let them know that we are not going to be messed with should they continue to pursue. Plot a second jump vector that will allow us to angle away from that ship while keeping our side deflectors to them. I don't want to test our weak ass on their technology should this get ugly."

Sharon nodded and began to calculate another exit point. While she waited on the numbers, she said, "I keep expecting to see a fleet of ships popping out of warp any minute now. They have been monitoring us for a while now." Having received the new calculations, she relayed the course headings to the navigator. The navigator entered the course correction into the navigation computer where it could be activated quickly. Sharon validated the entry and told Linda the new course was plodded and ready.

"Very well," Linda responded. "Let's also keep an eye on these other planets as we pass by, just in case they have a ship or two hiding behind them. I don't want them jumping out at us at the last minute."

❖ ❖ ❖

It had been several dozen beats since the message had been sent. So far, nothing new had developed with the other ship. Synska byf tried to give a relaxed appearance, even though he felt anything but relaxed. He was wondering if he should attempt to overtake the ship. He looked up at the view screen when the tracking overling said that the other ship had increased speed. The overlord was confused for a moment about what this meant. He wondered if he had just scared them off. Could they be testing him to see if he had enough speed to stay with them? The underlord broke his train of thought when he asked, "Do you recommend increasing speed to follow, Overlord?"

Making up his mind, synska byf responded, "Yes, underlord, increase speed to maximum."

Once the ship had reached top speed, brk'erst reviewed the tracking data and said, "I'm sorry, Overlord, we will not be able to match their current speed. They have a six-percent top speed advantage over us."

The other ship had put a lot of distance between them before the bfnor torrnt had come up to her top speed. Doing a quick calculation is his head, he determined that they were still within effective range for the energy beam, but he had his doubts about using it, thinking that this ship had effective shielding. He asked, "Underlord, have you determined if the energy readings surrounding the ship match the energy readings that surrounding the other object?"

Brk'esrt looked at the overlord and answered, "Yes, Overlord. The tracking overling has determined this ship and the object have the same energy signature. However, this ship has a stronger signature by nearly a factor of five."

"This would rule out our using the energy beam as long as that shielding is in place. Our only real option is to use a mine, which is not a very effective weapon to use against a moving ship," synska byf stated.

"The use of the mines would be limiting. If they veer away from a mine after we fire it, they will quickly learn that it can not track their movements," replied brk'erst.

Synska byf went through the possible options. His ship was nothing more than a minelayer. He liked to think it was more than that, but when it came down to it, the bfnor torrnt was made to lay and retrieve mines. Setting and retrieving buoys was a natural transition for this type of ship. The bfnor torrnt was not made to chase enemy ships and slug it out with them. Even its energy beam was designed to explode mines that had become too unstable to handle. He did not have any of the long-range weapons that the true fighting ships had. What he wouldn't give for a long reaching rocket right now. Just one keddrft jraatk, Stalking Death, rocket would stop that ship right in its tracks. "Assuming it could get through that shielding," he reminded himself. However, if he could fire a mine set with a proximity fuse, and get it close to the other ship's exhaust trail, he might be able to disable it. With the ship disabled, he could place additional mines around the ship to prevent it from leaving. Once a set of linked mines were in place, the ship would not be able to move without risking them being set off. With a little luck, he may even be able to reload and set up a second set outside of the first. The Council would look very favorable upon him were he to capture this ship without damaging it.

Synska byf turned to brk'erst saying, "Underlord, I am not going to let that ship get away from me. Have a proximity mine loaded into a front launch tube. Set it to run directly along the ship's current course. I want to get it close to the exhaust ports. Inform me when you are ready to launch."

"As you command, Overlord," brk'erst responded. He would never argue with his overlord, but he did not like taking a threatening action against this other ship. They had no way of knowing what it was capable of doing. It wanted to leave, and he thought they should let it go. Other than whatever information it recorded, it could only take back where it had been. It was reasonable to believe that this information was already known because he believed they had come here looking for the object that was destroyed. Now, if this ship failed to return, what would be the next logical step? Most likely a whole fleet of ships would arrive to investigate. If they let it leave, they could go back to say they were pursued, but that was all. They did not seem interested in harming the bfnor torrnt, so why provoke them? Brk'erst knew enough to keep these thoughts to himself as he waited. A signal light lit up reflecting that a connection had been made with the mine. The overling quickly entered the commands into the mine's onboard computer as the underlord relayed them. Completed, the overling sent a signal that would reflect on the status board in the forward launch room. This would let the overling there know that he could disconnect the connection cable and load the mine into the tube. An unlit light showed which launch tube was empty. He now waited for the status light to come on, showing that the mine was ready to launch.

When the status light lit up, Brk'erst informed the overlord, who ordered that the mine be launched. Brk'erst came alongside synska byf as they watched the mine shoot away from the front of the ship. They both observed the flash as the powerful thrusters came to life. The mine veered slightly until it was following the same course as the target. It became a black dot against the lighter hull color of the ship it was following.

"With a little luck, the mine might become lost in their exhaust signature and they may not be able to detect it. The shield energy should ignite it. I set the magnetic field at minimum to allow it to get as close as possible. If they detect it, they will probably just veer away from it," commented Brk'erst.

Synska byf only nodded his head at the underlord's comment. He knew that his decision to fire that mine was a huge step between trying to distract them and attempting to disable the ship. But, he also knew that his only hope was to try and outwit whoever was commanding that ship. He was counting on the element of surprise. Besides, they did almost run into a planet coming in. Perhaps they were not all that smart. He looked at the tracking display. The mine had already covered a third of the distance needed to reach the other ship, and they had yet to take any detectable corrective actions. Maybe he could sneak that mine right up their exhaust trail. As an afterthought, he said, "Reduce speed to half. We will back off a bit just in case this does not work."

The tracking specialist informed Sharon that the trailing ship had increased speed. When the speed had leveled off, it became apparent they would not overtake the Privateer.

Linda quietly watched the distance increase between the two ships. She was relieved to know that they were faster and would not have to worry about being overtaken before they reached their jump point. Now, it was just a matter of keeping watch on that ship to see what their next move would be, if any. Linda was tempted to jump from where they were, but that was too dangerous and, so far, not needed. Coming into this system just short of colliding with a planet made her cautious to trying anything rash.

Things had quieted down on the bridge as the Privateer continued pulling away from the other ship. They had passed the nearest planet, which had shown no hidden ships trying to head them off. Linda was just starting to breathe easy again.

The tracking specialist was first to detect the inbound object. This object was quite small compared to the trailing ship, but it appeared to have originated from it. She was sure that it was a weapon that had just been fired. She quickly marked the incoming object so the tracking computer would automatically feed data on its progress. She then turned to report. "Captain, I am picking up a small inbound object that was launched from that other ship! I believe it is a weapon! It is rapidly moving along our path to strike out aft end. I am relaying it to the forward view screen now."

Linda was startled by the specialist's report. The object was overtaking them at twice their current speed, according to the tracking information. Linda was glad she had kept her distance from that other ship. She had enough time to react to this threat. She was also disappointed that the other ship's captain had taken it to this level. This weapon did not appear to be just a warning shot.

In weapons control, Bill was already alerted to the incoming object. It had been picked up on passive tracking as soon as it left the other ship. He was not able to tell just what it was, but at the rate of speed it was traveling it could only be considered a weapon.

From the control console he switched targeting mode to active. This caused the object to display in red as it was bracketed in the tracking display. The turret, now linked with the fire control computer, swung around so the dual guns were pointed at the incoming object. The sound of the turret swinging on its track vibrated within the compartment. The object would be in optimal firing range in about forty seconds. After that, the computer would have to rotate the turret left and right slightly to allow each barrel to fire on the target. The weapon's tracking computer could compensate for that easily enough, Bill knew. He waited for the order he knew would come at any moment now.

Linda switched on her comm unit. "Mr. Launtra, this is the captain. We have an incoming object directly on our stern. You are cleared to fire with the intent to deter, disable, or destroy it."

Bill acknowledged the order and insured that the bridge tracking feed was active. He asked, "Mr. Bulloch, do you have a definite target lock on the object?"

"Yes, sir! Angle to the gun is true. Elevation to target is minus two degrees. Firing solution is true to target. No angle deflection is anticipated. We are ready to fire."

Bill took a quick look at the target tracking display and could see that the object was fast approaching the ultimate firing angle. He waited until the two lines representing each shot angle came close to intersecting on the target. He ordered, "Mr. Bulloch, single burst, both guns if you will."

Don Bulloch switched the firing selection to single burst mode without even taking his eyes of the targeting display. Don's training was kicking in. He was still receiving a clear targeting solution from the tracking computer. The object was bracketed in the target display by a red box with two yellow lines slowly coming together as the weapon closed in. This was an overhead view of the firing solution, and the yellow lines were the projected firing angles for the two guns. He flipped up a clear protection panel covering a red firing button with his thumb. When the two lines converged on the target, he pressed the button.

The hair on Bills arms reacted to the static buildup as the plasma energy routed through the conduits. Vents located aft of the gun turret opened to expel the heat buildup within the conduit casing. Like a lightning bolt, the plasma energy discharged into each gun pot. Plasma now built up inside each gun barrel waiting for the computer-controlled trigger that would send it on its way. A ball of plasma was expelled from the two gun barrels. First, the left barrel, then the right. The discharge was so rapid that, to Bill, it sounded like a single shot.

Both conduits in the compartment vibrated from the recoil of the turret guns. Looking at the rear display, he could see each burst of light as it rocketed away from the aft end of the ship. They looked like large shooting stars as they rapidly trailed away towards the oncoming target.

Once fired, the course of the plasma bolt could not be altered. The computer calculated the firing angle by factoring in the target's course and speed along with the ship's course and speed, factoring in any expected deviation from outside factors. A plasma bolt, once released, traveled at such speeds that the intended target had little time to react.

The plasma bolts stuck the object dead on, one right after the other. The plasma energy melted through the weapon so quickly that it ignited the explosives and propellant in a single blast. Bill looked away from the target display screen when it went very bright at the point of impact. He glanced at the tracking display to validate what he already knew. The object was no longer being tracked. He reported to the bridge, "Bridge, weapons control, the incoming object has been destroyed. Weapons tracking show all clear."

The communication specialist relayed, "Weapons control, bridge, we show the same. Captain relays a well done."

"Well that was a damn stupid thing for them to do! Do they think I am just going to sit here and let them take pot-shots at me? If they want to start playing dirty I can sure as hell give it back in kind," Linda said, more to herself than anyone. She was taking the attempt to harm her ship personally. As captain, she was responsible for the safety of the ship and all that served her.

Sharon looked at the target tracking display. She added, "They have slowed down. I assume to put a little distance between us and them. We still have nine hours to go before reaching a safe jump point."

"Nine hours is a long time to play cat and mouse with them. We need to send them a strong message that they best leave us be," Linda responded as she opened her comm link. "Mr. Launtra, this is the Captain. Is the ship within accurate firing range?"

Bill looked up at the targeting display before replying, "Yes, Captain, the ship is nearing the edge of our range. If they continue to fall back at their current pace, they will be out of range in about four and a half minutes."

"Bill, I intend to get that ship off our tail. I am authorizing you to fire on that ship. Give them a few shots to drive them off. We will monitor the results from here," Linda responded.

Linda asked to have the forward view display replaced with the targeting feed. This would mimic what was being fed into the targeting computer in weapons control. From her chair, she could override the firing controls if she needed to—a safety feature built into the weapon controls. Linda knew that Bill would follow her orders to the letter. She was not worried about having to override his commands.

The anger in the captain's voice surprised Bill. Normally, she projected a calm demeanor whenever she was on the bridge. Bill turned his focus to the orders he had just received. This was a serious matter. Fire on another ship went beyond the code of conduct within the merchant marines. In fact, the merchant marines pilot manual forbad any ship from firing on another without due cause. But, if this was not due cause, he was not sure what was. He expected some serious debriefing when they returned. If they returned, he reminded himself.

"Don, begin tracking the ship, passive only. I don't want to give them a warning we are locking onto them. Set the shot sequence at three bolts only. Stand by for my orders to fire. Be ready to have a firing solution calculated as soon as we go active. We'll switch status just prior to shooting," Bill ordered, as he turned his attention to the control console.

Linda watched the progress from the bridge. So far, everything she could see met with her approval. She silently applauded Bill's decision to stay passive while they set up for the firing solution.

"Don, go active and validate the firing solution. Fire as soon as validation is received," Bill commanded.

Don flipped up the protective cover on the firing button. He then nodded to Specialist Trium, who was sitting next to him, to switch to active. The blue box that bracketed the ship turned red, the white-lined shot paths turned yellow, and confirmation was received in the target computer. Don pressed the button as soon as the confirmation tone was heard.

The firing sequence was slower this time, as the computer had to allow for the turret to be aligned after each shot. The left barrel was fired first; the computer rotated the turret left slightly to align the right barrel, fired, and then rotated the turret right again to align the left barrel for the third and final shot. This was all accomplished within a single second. Bill and his crew heard each shot in quick succession.

❖ ❖ ❖

Synska byf watched the mine as it shot out from the front of his ship. It quickly corrected its course and sped away. The mine would run on this course until it ran out of propulsion or hit its target. He was hoping that they would not detect it quickly enough to take evasive action, at least not enough to prevent the mine from striking their shielding. He said to brk'erst, "If they saw it, they should take evasive action at any moment now."

They both began to grow hopeful as the mine drew closer and the ship had not taken any action. Brk'erst was still concerned about their firing at this ship. He was not sure this was the best thing to do. He continued to watch the forward view, even though he could not see anything. The mine was nothing more than a tiny dot now. He noticed a bright dot appear. It was traveling so fast that he did not have time to say anything before a flash was seen. The flash expanded into a slightly brighter flash before dying out completely. After a moment, he was once again looking out at the fleeing ship. The ship had pulled so far away he could barely make it out.

Neither said anything for a few beats. The overlord finally looked over at the tracking display and could see that the mine was no longer being tracked. It was now showing only the fleeing ship.

Brk'erst finally said, "If I had not seen this with my own eyes, I would not have believed it. A light fired directly into the path of our mine. I think we have just seen the effectiveness of that weapon we were wondering about. I only saw one light, but two explosions occurred."

The sudden loss of the mine had synska byf speechless for the moment. He looked at brk'erst and finally commented, "We would be wise to keep our distance from this ship. Reduce speed to one-quarter. I had not anticipated they would have the ability to track and destroy the mine.

I will need to come up with another way of slowing them down or distracting them long enough to allow our other ships to arrive. Any ideas, underlord?"

Even though brk'erst would rather have just let them go, he knew better than to contradict the wishes of the Council or his overlord. He wondered how many mines they could track and how quickly they could destroy them. That single mine had been over halfway there when it was destroyed. With this thought in mind, he responded, "What if we fired all the forward link mines, followed by a single proximity mine. We could have the link mines travel on various courses to bracket the ship while the proximity mine follows along their course. We could then explode the link mines one at a time. This may cause enough of a disruption to their sensor equipment to get the proximity mine through. As the link mines get closer, they should cause longer lasting disruptions. Our overling would have to react quickly to insure that we explode the link mines at the right intervals to prevent the other ship from destroying them first. We could take the timing of their first shot, reduce it by a specific factor, and then use that to determine the detonation timing. We may even be able to get a linked mine in close enough to weaken or eliminate that shield before the proximity mine reaches them."

No reply came from synska byf for several beats. Finally, he replied, "I think your idea is a sound one, underlord. Having all the link mines to deal with should help get that proximity mine in close. My only hesitation is that we will be firing at them with such force that they will have to respond. We will veer away once the last mine is fired. Have another proximity mine made ready. While that is going on, work with the overling to set up the link mines to launch as you suggested. Let me know when you are ready."

Brk'erst walked over to work with the overling to get the mines set up. It would take longer with the need to set the guidance on all the linked mines already sitting in the tubes. He watched the overling set each mine in turn while waiting for the ready light to display on the proximity mine. Fortunately, the linked mines could be adjusted in the tubes without having to remove them. This was proving to be a huge time saver at the moment. Brk'erst expected to have all the link mines ready to go before the proximity mine was ready to load into the one empty tube.

At the tracking station, v'sdntil continued to monitor the other ship's movements. He stiffened as he picked up a strange power spike on the sensor. He had never seen anything like it before. Just as he was going to inform the overlord of this, the tracking computer warned him of three high-energy readings being picked up. They were the same energy readings he had detected just prior to the mine's destruction. He quickly yelled out, "Three high-energy burst in route to the ship! Impact point is dead ahead!"

Synska byf looked up from the monitor at his side to look out at the forward view. He could see a bright shooting star coming directly at him. He knew there were two more behind this one from the overling's warning. Without hesitating, he ordered, "Hard right! Thirty degree down angle! Ahead full, emergency power!"

He knew his ship would not be able to turn in time to avoid being hit. His only hope now was to spread the hits along the upper hull of the ship, rather than take them all on the bow. He could feel the ship slide over and begin to dip, but the movement would not be enough. The incoming ball of light was going to hit them on top of the bridge. He grabbed the chair arms to brace for the impact. He leaned over in a subconscious effort to speed the ship's movement.

While the bfnor torrnt did not have shielding, sysnka byf was now relying on the thick double hull construction of the old style krracts design. He knew his ship was built to take punishment in the event of an accidental explosion when working with mines, especially in the early days when mines were very unreliable. The first shot hit directly over the bridge, where it impacted with the thick outer hull. The plasma blast spent its energy on the outer hull before dissipating in the space between the inner and outer hulls. Everyone on the bridge was knocked to the deck. The force caused the already dipping ship to nose downward at a quicker pace. This downward push saved the lives of all those on the bridge, as the second bolt struck further aft. The impact extended the outer hull damage from forward of the bridge down nearly half of the ship's length. This second bolt did not penetrate the second hull before dissipating. However, it did caused the ship to buck into a level position, thereby allowing the third bolt to pass through the missing outer hull section and strike the inner hull near the center of the ship. The resulting energy blast breached the inner hull directly above the large machine shop.

Exposed to the vacuum of space, the ship's large machine shop was stripped of everything that wasn't securely fastened down. Eight underlings, along with the overling supervising them, were plucked out the hull opening. With no collision alarm sounded, the hatchways leading into the compartment were still open. This allowed for the vacuum of space to enter adjacent compartments as well. The adjoining storage compartment further aft began spilling out raw building materials used within the machine shop. These large chucks of metal blocks tore sections from the hatch opening as they passed through. They also caused further damage to the inner hull as they pounced their way out of the ship. The large access hatch over the top of the storage compartment was blown open with such force that one of the hatch covers was ripped off its hinges. Both compartments were now completely exposed to the vacuum of space. The hatchway door on the opposite bulkhead of the storage compartment buckled inward, but held. In the compartment on the opposite side of the machine shop was the main power relay center. All power from the large generators located four decks down was funneled through the breakers in this compartment. The open hatch allowed the vacuum of space to suck out everyone and everything through the open hatchway. Flying objects struck the large circuit panels as they passed by. Cracked circuit breakers shorted out across other circuits causing a massive explosion throughout all the panels. The resulting fire began to melt wiring. The massive generators began to overload, causing them to shut down. The entire inside of the ship went dark. The fire within the power relay station died down quickly as the lack of air would not support it. Several smaller fires continued in stubborn defiance, as they fed on the air being sucked through small openings where the conduits passed through the decking and bulkheads.

One deck below the main relay station, air screamed though the conduit fittings. As the emergency lights came on, an overling directed some of the underlings to stuff whatever they could find around the leaking seals, while another overling hunted for some emergency wadding used to repair small hull breaches. The overling also ordered the hatches closed and sealed in case the bulkhead gave way. With the hatches closed, the vacuum was drawing out air faster than the air duct could replace it. The overling knew that stuffing objects into the spaces around the conduits and couplings was their only hope.

As the emergency lights came on in the engine room, the overling in charge came to his feet, slowly looking around. Without power, the ship could not be controlled. He noticed that the large cooling pumps had stopped. These cooling pumps were critical in keeping the main propulsion systems from overheating. They would have to manually shut down the feed lines to prevent each of the power plants from reaching critical mass and exploding. He ran over to one of the manual control wheels and began to rotate it as fast as he could. He yelled at underlings to do the same to the other control wheels. One by one, the main injection valves were closed off, and the five main feed lines to each propulsion unit were sealed. The overling watched as the hydraulic and pressure-sensitive gauges began a slow decent to zero. The temperature gauges held steady just below red line. He knew the propulsion units were hot, but at least they would not have been damaged. On each side of the compartment, an underling was standing by the emergency release levers in case they had to flood the compartment with coolant. They all understood that if those levers were released, all in the compartment would perish. But, to allow the propulsion units to overheat and explode would kill them and everyone else on the ship.

Synska byf came to his feet shortly after the emergency lights came on. Everything was out. He had no control over the ship and was running blind. The overlord was so in-tune with his ship that he could sense the difference in its sounds and vibrations. He knew from the various shakes and vibrations that they were in trouble. He watched as brk'erst came to his feet. A streak of blood was flowing down the side of his face. He sported a nasty gash on the top of his head. It was obvious that he had struck something when he was tossed off his feet. The overlord walked over to help his underlord steady himself. It had to have been a heavy blow to penetrate his thick hide. Brk'erst nodded, showing that he was okay, but he still looked shaken

"They have done a number on us. I need you to take a damage report throughout the ship and report back to me." The overlord guided brk'erst to the emergency exit ladder. It would lead him to the ship's main passageway. He knew the underlord would check out the vital areas first and report what he found.

As synska byf watched brk'erst leave, he felt the reduction in vibration as his ship lost momentum. He could tell that the main drive engines were shutting down. He knew that power was needed to keep the coolant flowing. He was thankful that someone down there was taking care of the propulsion units. He hated being blind. He had a ship out there that had hit him hard. He knew that if power was not restored soon, they were as helpless as a ling. He thought to himself that he should have known something like this might happen. Would he have let a ship fire on him without returning fire? He was beginning to doubt his ability to command. So far, he had not been able to determine the strategy of the other ship's commander. Everything he had done so far had not produced the results he'd expected. Well, orders or not, he was done with it. He even wished the other ship would finish them off to save him the embarrassment of having to face the Council. The overlord knew that he had made the most underling of mistakes. He had under estimated his prey. He had assumed that when they came in close to that planet, that the commander must have been inexperienced. He was paying for that overconfidence now and he knew it.

Linda watched as the three bright flashes appeared on the rear display. It was apparent that all three had hit the ship. She listened as the specialist relayed their interpretation of the sensor data coming in.

"Sensors reporting a rapid decline in power readings. Sensors are picking up increased heat signatures in the propulsion output. Heat signatures are rising. Propulsion output is declining at a steady pace. Heat signatures are steadying up. Propulsion is out. The ship is drifting along on its original course, but they are beginning to fall off a bit. Power output is too low for sensors to detect. Heat signatures are declining also."

Linda tried to make sense out of the reports she was hearing. It sounded like the ship had been hit hard enough to require a shutdown of the propulsion units. She was sure they had knocked out the ship's power source. The sensors had recorded the loss of power before the propulsion systems began declining. She now wondered if they had hit an unshielded ship. She knew the damage a plasma bolt could inflict on an unprotected hull. If all three bolts had hit an unshielded ship in the same spot, they could drive deep within a ship. From what she could tell from the tracking display, they had hit the ship head on as she attempted to turn. She wondered if the first bolt had hit the bridge, while the other two followed behind it to drive ever deeper into the ship. The third shot may have made it to the engine room. She cringed at that thought.

"All stop!" the captain ordered.

Sharon looked at the captain and questioned, "Captain?"

The captain looked directly at her second-in-command and said, "It is very apparent that we have hurt that ship. We may have even put it out of action for good. I do not want to live my life wondering if we abandoned a crew out here to die from exposure. Without power, they will not be able to maintain atmosphere for long." She looked over at the tracking station and asked, "What's the status of the other ship?"

A tracking specialist answered, "They are currently on a zero, eight, eight course heading with a negative two degree down drift. Their drift rate is sixty-eight hundred meters per minute. Propulsion emission is negligible. No detectable energy readings. They appear to be dead in space, Captain."

Linda again looked at the tracking display. "Commander, turn us around. Let's go have a look. Set an intercept course. Half speed ahead."

After relaying the captain's orders, Sharon spoke to her in a low voice, "Captain, they could be trying to trick us by drawing us in closer. The closer we get, the less reaction time we will have should they fire another one of those missile-type weapons of theirs. Do you think this is wise?"

"No I don't think this is wise. But, I have to live with myself. I want to be sure we don't leave an entire crew to die. If they are okay but without life support, we need to offer some kind of aid. Even if we just transfer over one of our surface generators. Maybe an offer of kindness will defuse this whole situation and lead to some good out here. I am willing to take the risk and live with the consequences. From what I am hearing, I doubt that this is a trick."

Sharon didn't really care a whole lot about what may or may not happen with those on the damaged ship. She wanted to get out of here. Turning back was not to her liking. She said, "I understand the concern, Captain, but I am obligated to remind you that our orders were specific about our leaving without delay."

"Your concern and reminder has been noted, Commander. I am willing to take full responsibility for this decision. I know you are doing your job, Sharon, so let's not have any further discussion on this here."

"As you wish, Captain." Sharon reluctantly returned to her duty of insuring the captain's orders were being carried out. She had done her job by reminding the captain of their orders. The ship completed a reversal of course, and they were heading back towards the stricken ship. Sharon was sure that Linda was going to get them all killed.

Even though the other ship was drifting slightly away from the Privateer, they were able to catch up to it in short order. The captain ordered, "Stand off at one kilometer. Place us on a parallel track. Match up course and speed."

Linda looked over the damaged ship and commented, "Those bolts sure decimated their hull. The rest of the ship seems intact, though. I would expect that they should be able to do some damage control. The least we can do now is stop their drift so they can tackle repairs on a more stable ship."

Sharon nodded and replied, "Two shuttles should be able to do the trick." And the sooner the better, she thought.

"I agree. See to it. I don't want to hang around here any longer than we have to. Once we have them stopped, we will see what other aid we can provide before heading out again," Linda ordered.

Two shuttles were sent out, each with a pilot and a spotter to help in working the shuttles into place. Each shuttle sped around to the front of the damaged ship and turned to face it. The shuttles reversed their speed to match that of the drifting ship, backing off power until they came to rest against the forward hull. Once both shuttles were nose to nose with the hull, they began to slowly apply forward thrust. Being careful not to apply thrust too quickly or out of sequence with each other, they slowly but surely brought the ship to a halt. They backed away and headed back to the Privateer.

Linda said to Sharon, "As soon as both shuttles are on board again, let's take another assessment of their damage. I would like to offer more aid, but I am at a loss as to how we can do that without giving them the wrong impression. This whole affair has been one misstep after another. I would like to get a top down look at the hull damage. This will give me a good idea just how far our shots penetrated."

The tracking specialist reported, "Captain, I am showing an increase in energy readings. It appears they are restoring power. I am not reading any propulsion output as of yet."

Linda looked over at Sharon and said, "They appear to be recovering well enough for now. Let's get turned around and headed out of here as soon as the shuttles are aboard. I want to put a lot of distance between us and them, as fast a possible."

Brk'erst returned from his inspection of the ship and began to run through the damage assessment with synska byf. "Overlord, here is where we are at. The hull has been breached somewhere near or above the machine shop. I suspect that the top loading hatches may have been blown open. Without power, I can not verify this. I do know that the machine shop, the main repair storage hold, and the main power relay stations are exposed to space. All the hatches leading into those compartments are showing vacuum stress. I have an overling supervising a working party to shore them up. The damage control board indicates a fire warning for the main relay compartment, but I suspect that the fire would have died out by now. The main generators automatically shut down, so no damage to them occurred. The underlings have been working on sealing off the vacuum leaks to the adjoining compartments and are just about done. I have underlings working on getting our backup relay station on line. They should have it up shortly. We can then bring the generators back on line and restore power. The main propulsion units are undamaged, but restarting them will take a little longer once power is restored. They had to manually shut down the power feeds, so they will have to manually reopen them again."

Synska byf was pleased to hear that they would have power soon. He did not like being blind. He had no idea what was going through the minds of whoever controlled that other ship. He only hoped that they had just kept going. As he returned to his chair, he felt the ship's forward momentum slacking. He questioned, "We appear to be braking. How is this possible?"

Brk'erst only shook his head. He was also confused as to why the ship would be slowing its drift. It wasn't long before they could sense that the ship had stopped and was now floating in space. He could tell that they were beginning to spin slowly. He also noticed that he was getting lighter. The emergency gravity wells were beginning to fail. They would all be floating around soon if power wasn't restored. Normally, they could rely on the emergency energy packs for days, but, with the relay station down, each component was running on its own internal power backup. They only lasted a few hours at the most.

"Is it possible that the other ship has arrived and is holding us for boarding? I want you to gather up as many underlings as you can spare. Take up a position between the main passageway and the bridge. If they try to board us, I will rely on you to prevent them from reaching the bridge," replied synska byf.

The overhead lighting came back on just as brk'erst started to leave. Synska byf told him to wait a beat. Slowly, each system began to come back up. The overlord ordered the front display to be reset as soon as the sensor initialized. The forward display began to show color, and then images began to appear. They both watched as two small shuttles could be seen speeding away from the ship. The sensor picked up the other ship standing off the left side. The viewer was altered to show the ship. Synska byf asked to have the view magnified by four. They were now getting the best view of the ship since it had arrived. The two shuttles came back into view and nearly blocked the entire screen. The shuttles returned to the rear of the ship and disappeared into the hull. It was hard for synska byf to detect the shuttle bay openings from the angle they were at, but he could still just barely see them. Soon, the opening disappeared as the hatch doors slid shut.

 Synska byf started running contingency plans through his mind. He could fire a mine, but only after he rotated the ship to point a launch tube in the right direction. He could not rotate the ship without propulsion. But, he could be ready for when propulsion returned. He asked, "Underlord, had you completed your work on that proximity mine before we were hit?"

 "No, Overlord. The mine had not been connected yet. I would also have to recalculate the firing angles again."

 Synska byf hesitated and then replied, "Set up the proximity mine to fire at that ship. If we can get propulsion back quick enough, we may be able to turn and fire at them before they can board us. It would be impossible for them to track and destroy a mine at this close a range."

 Brk'erst just couldn't keep quiet any longer. He came closer to his overlord saying quietly, "Do you think it is wise to take such a risk. If we can not disable them completely, another hit from that weapon of theirs could blow out the hatches in the damaged compartments. Also, any damage to our backup power relay station would leave us without power for quite a while. We would be hard pressed to regain power before our reserves ran out on life support and gravity."

"I understand your concern, underlord. I am not going to fire unless I think they intend to board us. Once we get our propulsion back on line, I intend to back away to a safer distance. Until then, let's see what external damage we have."

Brk'erst relayed the order to the overling to continue to set up the proximity mine and to reset the firing angles on the link mines as well. He then returned to his overlord's side. Together, they watched as the external cameras were activated. They knew the ship was struck on the top, so they started with the cameras covering that area. Both were not surprised to see the top hatchway covers were blown open. On one of the hatches, seven of the eight hinges had pulled away from the ship. The single hinge, still holding on, was bent severely while the hatch cover itself was nowhere to be seen. Synska byf commented that it must have drifted past when the ship was stopped. The other hatch cover had folded over nearly in half. Neither expected to see damage to the extent they were seeing on the outer hull. Both were feeling fortunate to be alive at this moment. They could not see the damage forward of the machine shop area because the camera in that location was not working. Synska byf commented that the camera had probably been either blown off or damaged when the hatch broke free.

As he reviewed the damage, synska byf said, "Underlord, I think it would be a good idea if you inspected the inner hull from here to the power relay station. Let me know if you find internal structural damage that needs immediate attention. I am going to find out how soon we will have propulsion again."

As brk'erst left the bridge, synska byf communicated with his engineering overling. He received word that the propulsion units were coming on-line now. He could begin to feel the vibration under his feet as the massive units began to come to life again. He always thought how impressive it was to be able to feel the propulsion units considering they were located deep within the ship. He also noticed that the other ship had turned away and was heading back out again.

"Begin pulling away from them. Slow and easy, I do not want to alarm them any sooner than we have to," synska byf ordered. He wondered if they picked up his energy readings and decided to put some distance between them. He ordered the ship turned to bring the forward tubes to bear on the other ship. He was not going to take any chances. He also didn't miss the fact that both of those massive barrels were pointed directly at his ship. He had learned the hard way that those barrels represented some devastating firepower.

chapter eight

The shuttles were secured to the mooring cleats in the shuttle bay just as the Privateer got under way again. The captain had been notified that sensors were showing an increase in propulsion emissions from the other ship. The Privateer was just beginning to put some distance between them when word came that the other ship was moving.

Linda watched as it slowly backed away while turning to become head-on to her ship. She didn't like the idea of that ship facing her again. She could only hope that she had shown them that she would not hesitate to protect her ship, while also showing she would not harm them further, unless provoked. They must have known that she could have finished them off quite easily while they were immobilized.

Sharon leaned toward Linda and said, "If they fire another one of those weapons of theirs, we will not be able to stop it at this range. Let's pray they don't decide to take another shot at us."

Keeping her eyes on the view screen, Linda responded, "So far, they seem willing to let us leave. I don't want to do anything to cause them to have doubts. I am concerned that they were able to get power so soon. They must have suffered damage to something other than their propulsion to be underway so fast. Our bolts must not have penetrated as deeply as we first feared. This is both good and bad. We may not have inflicted as much damage as we first feared, so they should be able to return home.

However, we now have a frightened, if not angry, enemy on our hands. I intend to be very careful from here on out."

Linda sat back in her command chair to activate a comm link. When Bill answered, she said, "Bill, keep a sharp eye out for another launch of one of their weapons. You have permission to take them out as soon as you detect them."

After confirming the order, Bill returned to his tracking of the other ship. He had the weapons control on active tracking to keep a target lock on the ship. He wanted to insure the gun stayed on target, and, hopefully, the captain of the other ship would notice it.

Synska byf watched in silence as the other ship sped away. As the ship turned, light was projected into one of the barrels. What he saw surprised him. The light was reflecting on what appeared to be glass panels. Each panel started out wide against the inside of the barrel and then corkscrewed around and outwards to join with a long metal rod, narrowing as it went. The panels were deep within the barrel, while the rod ran right down the center of the barrel to stop a short distance from the barrel's outlet. The light leaving the barrel brought him out of his amazed wonderment.

He quickly calculated how far the two ships were apart and how fast a mine would reach them. He doubted they could track and destroy a mine at this range. But, what if the mine did not knock out the ship's ability to fire back. Sure, he may knock out the propulsion, but, if they could still fire, he would be powerless to prevent it. He also had to consider that they were ready to fire at his ship on a moment's notice. Even if he fired a mine and it got through, they would have time to fire at him before the mine reached its target. At the current angle of both ships, those energy bursts would hit directly on top again. "That two-headed beast shoots very deadly fire," he told himself. He would not be able to maneuver the ship very quickly at their current slow rate of speed, so dodging a return shot would be impossible.

The overling reported that the linked mines were ready to fire and the proximity mine was being loaded into the tube. Shortly after, brk'erst returned to the bridge to report, "There appears to be only slight damage to the inner hull between here and the power relay station. It has bulged outward slightly, but it appears to be sound enough. I was not able to detect any vacuum leaks."

"Very good, underlord. We will have all our mines ready to fire shortly," replied synska byf.

What to do next was nagging at synska byf. He was under way again, had full power, and had a full compliment of mines ready to be launched. He could chance firing at this ship, but at what risk? Looking at the display, he could see they had doubled the distance already. He did not know how much more damage the inner hull could take behind them…and what about the hatches? Would they hold if the ship were shaken about? He wasn't even sure he could harm the other ship. He would be taking an incredible risk. But, his orders were to prevent this ship from leaving until help arrived. He watched as the distance continued to mount between the two ships. He was quickly losing the advantage of his mines as the distance between them increased. He started to think about his own ship and the damage they had sustained. How could he return to face the Council with this much damage and having nothing to show for it? The more he thought about it, the more he became convinced he needed to make that other ship pay. He had made up his mind: he was not going to let them just leave after damaging his ship. Would he stop hunting a prey just because it bit him?

"Underlord, I want you to fire that proximity mine followed by a linked mine. Fire them so they are only a beat apart," Synska byf ordered sharply.

Noting the tone in the overlord's voice, brk'erst knew better than to say anything. He watched over the overling as he selected the firing sequence. He quickly validated the tube carrying the proximity mine had been selected to launch first. He knew that if this did not work, they would not survive any return fire. The overlord was placing the ship and the lives of all on board in danger with his actions. It had come down to an all or nothing response. Once the entries were completed, he told synska byf that they were ready to fire.

Brk'erst walked over to the overlord and said, "We will not be able to withstand much more punishment, especially if we take another hit on the upper hull." He knew that the overlord was not going to be swayed now that he was angry, but he felt compelled to say something.

"Underlord, I understand your concern. I do not believe they can target and destroy two mines at this distance. If we can get one to explode close enough to put them out of action for a while, we can get the upper claw in this situation," synska byf replied. Looking back at the weapons station, he ordered, "Launch both mines. One beat apart." He then looked back at his underlord and stated, "If we can knock the shielding out, we may be able to disable the gun with our energy weapon. Have the overling target the turret and prepare to fire on my orders. If we are going to die, we will die on our own terms."

The bridge shook as the first mine was launched, followed shortly by a second launching. Brk'erst watched the weapons overling as he targeted the turret with the primary weapons system. He glanced up to see how the mines were progressing.

"Captain, I am picking up two objects fired from the other ship! They are tracking directly on our stern! Time to impact, eleven seconds!" shouted the tracking specialist.

Linda's instincts took over as she began rattling off orders. She knew there was no time to try picking them off. "Hard over starboard, take us up! Ahead full!" If nothing else, she would present them with the top and side deflectors rather than the rear ones.

Bill had just received a target lock on the first weapon when the Privateer's sharp turn caused them to lose it again. He quickly tried to regain the lock. He had hoped to knock out one of them, but that was lost now.

Synska byf watched as the ship turned sharply and began to rise. Looking at the tracking display, he could see that they could not avoid setting off the proximity mine with its wide magnetic detection field. It should be close enough to shake them up. The second mine would fall farther behind with less effect. He doubted they could cause the damage he was hoping to inflict. He decided the best thing to do now was to get distance between his ship and theirs.

"Left full, ahead emergency power! Keep displaying the target as we turn," synska byf ordered. The first mine exploded as he expected. The blinding light made watching impossible. He counted one beat and ordered the linked mine to be set off. Another blinding flash filled the screen. He could hear the damaged upper hatch lid hitting the hull as they turned, followed closely by the shock waves from the two explosions.

Linda grabbed the chair arms as an explosion rocked the ship. Crew members were thrown all about the bridge. Then, a second explosion rocked the ship again, but with much less severity. Sparks flew as fuses blew out to protect delicate circuits. Display screens were going dark all over the bridge. Linda looked about and could see that they had lost tracking and sensors. She glanced at the damage control boards to see the deflector status. The rear and lower starboard deflectors were out. She closed her eyes and quickly thanked God the navigation system was still working.

"Hard about helm. Bring us back on course. Level off and head for the jump point. Best speed." She could feel a vibration under her feet as the ship banked hard left to return to their original course. In the rear display, she could see that they were venting steam out the exhaust ports. She expected a call from engineering any minute now asking to reduce speed. She would buy every extra second she could. She also struggled with the thought of firing back. Her knee-jerk reaction was to order Bill to fire, but she had been through that once already. If nothing else, she had learned that these weapons didn't appear to have tracked her ship as it turned. The two objects had continued straight without trying to follow her evasive maneuver. She now knew how to avoid them. She also knew that the more distance they put between the two ships, the more likely they could pick off any others. She nodded when Sharon reported that the other ship had taken evasive action and was moving away from them.

As Linda looked around, she could see that the specialists were already pulling panels to get under each station to replace fuses. Most of the circuits were too sensitive to rely on circuit breakers, so they used quick-acting fuses instead. Extra fuses were kept on the inside access covers so they could be replaced quickly. She found that her own monitor was still working, so she replayed the tracking information that was recorded in the ship's log. The recording confirmed her suspicions. The weapons they'd fired had run hot, straight, and normal. If she had not been moving almost straight away from the other ship, she could have outmaneuvered the weapons easily. Now, with each passing second, she was putting valuable distance between herself and that other ship. With tracking and sensors down, she could only see where the other ship was through the rear image feed. But, as the distance increased between the two ships, she was fast losing sight of it. Soon, she would not be able to detect if they fired anymore weapons.

Switching on the comm unit, Linda hailed emergency control. "Lieutenant, this is the captain. Is your sensor display working back there?"

Rebecca wasted little time in replying that their sensor display was out. This meant that the sensor control unit was down. Linda had little doubt that the specialists would have sensors back soon.

She then switched comm channels to weapons. "Bill, do you have tracking capability on the target?"

Bill was still tracking the other ship, but now in passive mode. He had checked his active capability right after the two explosions, but found that it was out. He had his specialist looking for the cause. He suspected that they had blown the fuse to it. He replied, "Yes, Captain. We are still tracking the target, but only passive mode is working at the moment. I can still fire the weapon on manual if need be. The targeting scope is undamaged."

The captain was relieved. They weren't completely blind then. With the weapon's tracking computer, they could keep an eye on the ship until the sensors came back on line. She said, "Commander, our sensor array is down. What is the current position and heading of the target?"

"The target is moving away on course three, oh, six. They are about forty-six kilometers heading away. Their speed is twenty-six thousand meters per minute. They are well within weapons range," Bill replied.

"Very well, Commander. Keep an eye on our target, but make periodic sweeps until our sensors are on line again."

Bill answered back, "Will do, Captain. We hope to have active tracking back in a few minutes."

Weapons Specialist Mila Heirlein took over as the other specialists were tracking down the problem. She was given the responsibility of cycling the passive display through a three hundred sixty degree sweep every thirty seconds. They always started and stopped on the target ship, which was still showing no signs of altering course. The tracking system used a specialized scanner that sat on top of the turret. Its sole function was to lock onto specific targets and feed input data back to the targeting computer. It was designed to be independent of the main sensors. Mila was on her ninth sweep when the target sensor picked up several objects. They were on the very edge of the weapon's sensor range, heading in system. She notified Bill, who confirmed the sightings through the target scope.

The bfnor torrnt was hard over when the explosive aftermath dissipated. Looking at the view screen, synska byf could see that the other ship was veering back toward its prior course. They had guessed right and they did not appear to be any worse for wear. Synska byf had had enough of this ship. It was a tough vessel with a nasty stinger. He was not going to mess with it anymore. He ordered the ship to be kept on its current course and decided he was going to leave it there until that other ship was gone. There was no doubt in his mind that the commander of the other ship now knew how to evade these mines. He knew that any edge he may have had was gone. They were too far apart now to attempt to shoot anymore mines that could not be easily outmaneuvered. He did notice that they were venting a little from the rear. He suspected that they were overheating their propulsion units to gain distance. He hoped they would have to slow down considerably until they cooled down. It would give more time for the other ships to arrive.

With the outer hull damage and the weakened inner hull, bfnor torrnt was only able to maintain two-thirds of its normal top speed. This concerned synska byf because he knew that they would have to crawl back to the spaceport without light speed. The stress of passing in and out of it could prove too much for the weaken sections of the ship. He would have to report this back to the Council and ask for permission to return home for repairs.

Brk'erst had moved away from the weapons station when it was apparent that he would not be needed there. He was thankful for that. He joined the overlord. Synska byf sensed his arrival and said, "I am through stalking this prey. They have convinced me that our ship is no match for their technology. It is too risky to keep trying to block their departure. I am not even sure what else we could do at this point. We are down one-third in top speed, outgunned, and badly damaged. If they want to go away, by the creator, I will let them go."

The overlord sat heavily in his chair. He was sure that this was the last time he would be in charge of a ship of his own. He doubted if he would ever be assigned to another ship again. They both watched as the troublesome ship continued to fade from the view screen to where it was finally replaced with the tracking feed. The overlord decided that if the damage to his ship didn't convince the Council that he tried all he could, then probably nothing short of their destruction would.

After a long silence, brk'erst said, "What I would not have given to see who was on that ship. We could have learned a lot from that technology. They were a very worthy adversary." Secretly though, he was glad that the overlord had finally decided to leave them alone. He wasn't sure why, but he actually felt sorry for them. They didn't seem to have done anything to deserve the actions the overlord was ordered to take. He just hoped that these other beings wouldn't come back later, in massive numbers, wanting revenge for what happened here today.

When there was no response from the overlord. Brk'erst continued thinking about what was waiting for them when they returned home. This was a first contact for them. They had not fared well in the encounter. He had no idea how the Council would react to what had happened. He suspected that they would have to give more thought to defense and their program on space travel.

An overling broke the silence by announcing, "Tracking is picking up five ships coming into the system." After a short pause, he continued, "Identification signatures are coming in now. They are the ghontuf, piirfh njyfn, tuilmf, njyfur lguunc, and the kaffnur dneui."

The overlord smiled. "Now we will see what they can do against our real fighting ships."

Synska byf wondered who the Council had managed to find as the command overlord. He knew that this alien ship was up against two cruiser-class vessels in the ghontuf, Slayer, and the piirfh njyfn, Wicked Bite. The njyfur Iguunc, Biting Prey, and the kaffnur dneui, Stalking Kill, were destroyer class ships that would provide support for the cruisers. The last ship was the tuilmf, Tracker, a fast attack destroyer—smaller than the other two destroyers, but more fleet of foot. The two cruisers were the newest ships in an aging fleet.

Brk'erst glanced up at the view screen, now showing the inbound track of the five ships. They were on an intersecting course with the fleeing ship. He was sure that the incoming fleet could cut off its escape. It would be close, of that he was sure. He thought it curious that the fleeing vessel was not altering course to turn away from them. He wondered if those creatures had any fear at all. Do they not understand fear, he wondered. Did death mean as little to them as it did to him a moment ago? He now wanted this ship captured intact. For no other reason than to see these most interested beings.

"They have exited at the best possible location to capture this ship," Brk'erst commented. He then added, "The tuilmf is falling off its course a little. I suspect that they are going to cut in behind to prevent them from reversing course. The kaffnur dneui is also falling off now. They appear to be trying to box them in on two sides."

They both watched as the njyfur iguunc took up the lead of the remaining three ships with the cruisers trailing behind and on each side of the destroyer. The destroyer was faster than the cruisers and slowly pulled away in a faster pursuit of the alien ship. He wondered how long it would be before the ship simply veered away from the oncoming krracts ships. He knew from having chased them that, unless they had more speed available, they could never hope to outdistance the destroyers. The cruisers were slower, but they had the angle to overtake them as it sat now. If they turned, he suspected that the tuilmf would drift to the left side and the kaffnur dneui would drop in behind, leaving the njyfur iguunc on the right side, along with the two cruisers. Sysnka byf now had the satisfaction of knowing that the overheating he has caused on that ship might prove to be their undoing. If they can't slow down, they will damage their drive unit and become an easy capture.

"Turn us about, underlord. Set a course to keep us on the inner-rim side of that ship. If they veer away, we should be able to gain ground. Reload the two front tubes with proximity mines," the overlord ordered excitedly. He was regaining his confidence. He couldn't catch up with the alien ship now, but maybe they would come to him trying to evade the others. He listened with satisfaction as the loose upper hatch slammed against the hull as they changed course. He told himself that he was going to make them pay for that, if he got the chance again.

Linda had been silent ever since she received word of the newly arrived ships. The sensors were coming online again, and the tracking display had been reset. As the data began to display, she could see they had no hope of reaching the initial jump point. With the speed of the three smaller ships fed into the tracking computer, she knew that they could not reach their secondary jump point before being overtaken if they turned. Turning was not her best option, as she saw it, as this would put the recently repaired rear deflectors toward the oncoming ships. Those shields were already shaky as it was without factoring in the abuse they had already taken. However, the two larger ships were traveling about the same speed as the Privateer, so if she turned, she would only have to deal with the other three. But, she was sure that these ships were here to stop her from leaving and most likely had the firepower to match that intent. She had made up her mind that she would continue on her course and let them make the first move. Looking at the tracking display again, she could tell that the lead ship of the group of three would pass in front of her position before she would reach the jump point. With the larger ships trailing, they would be just short of cutting across her path. On the plus side though, the damage she feared on the propulsion was not that severe. The engineers were pretty sure they could fix the problem without having to take any of the units off line.

Continuing to study the tracking display, she could see that two of the smaller ships were tacking slightly off the other three. She was sure that they were attempting to come in behind her and to the rear right of her. This left the other three to continue on in an attempt to block her path. She was now trying to decide what her best options were. She swore to herself as a reminder that she did not have the military experience for this kind of thing. How she would have loved to have had Bill on the bridge instead of Sharon. But she needed Bill at the guns, so that option was out. Sharon was worthless in this situation. She was on her own and feeling very inadequate at the moment.

The problem, as she saw it, was what the lead ship would do when it crossed her path. Maybe she should jump early. The picture of that planet in their path made her hesitate on that idea. They had calculated an exit point that would take them back home. She did not have the luxury of using the entry calculation, as they were not following that same path back out. That would have been the best choice. Jump directly back along the entry path for about ten minutes and then exit out to recalculate for the jump home. To do that, they would have to make a curved jump, which was not a safe option. Being even a hundredth of a degree off at light speed could plant them four miles deep into a planet's surface. The jump coordinates for this area were sketchy. The computer only had the original jump points calculated from the last known position of the probe. She would be jumping blind if she deviated from these known coordinates.

As the scenario unfolded, Linda and Sharon watched the results on the view screen. The smallest ship had fallen off the Privateer's stern and was turning to pursue. It was within firing range of the Privateer's guns, as were the two smaller ships. The two larger vessels would be within range in about six minutes. Linda was not going to fire unless they fired first. She was also not going to slow down or stop to give them a chance to completely box her in. She liked having her port side open in case she needed some room to maneuver. Currently, only the ship at her stern could fire at the weaker rear deflectors.

Linda switched on her comm unit and said, "Mr. Launtra, keep a track on the lead ship, A1. If we must fire, I want to open a hole between the jump point and us. Also, keep a secondary target track on the trailing ship, A3. If they open fire, I want to be able to take it out, should they begin to penetrate our rear deflectors."

Sharon waited for Bill to acknowledge before she interrupted. "Captain, damage control reports that the starboard deflectors are back on line. The Privateer is one hundred percent operational again. Engineering reports that the main inductors are back to normal cooling, so full speed can be maintained. Weapons control reports that both capacitors are at full charge with both generators operating within tolerable limits. Active tracking is on line again."

"Very well, Commander," Linda replied. Both knew that the captain had access to the same information that

Sharon was providing, but having it heard out loud might ease some of the tension from the crew on the bridge.

"Captain, the damaged ship has altered course and is currently on a zero, one, four heading. I have placed its course angle on the display," commented the tracking specialist. "They are still traveling at a reduced speed. I relabeled this ship A6 so the new incoming ships would be A1 through A5."

The tracking display was providing Linda with a view of all ships in motion. With her ship in the center of the display, the other ships were displayed with letter and number sequences. They ranged from A1 through A6. Each symbol had a tracking line showing its direction, with the course and speed displayed below the line. This helped Linda keep track of what was happening all around her ship.

The Privateer shook slightly. The tracking specialist reported, "A1 has fired a shot in front of us. Some kind of energy stream. It glanced off the very edge of the forward deflectors."

The tracking display was showing a black dotted line that traced the path of the shot fired by the lead ship. Linda said to Sharon, "A shot across the bow. Well, they have asked us to stop and lower our flag, Commander. What do you suggest we do?"

"Maybe we should ask them to surrender," she said with a smile. When the captain didn't respond in kind she added, "I recommend we fire a warning shot of our own to show our intent to continue on our way."

The captain replied, "Agreed. Be ready in case we need to perform some emergency course changes. I intend to keep our side shields toward them as much as possible."

Opening a comm channel to weapons, Linda asked, "Mr. Launtra, would you be so kind as to fire a warning shot across the bow of target A1, please? Thank you, Commander."

Bill followed the order.

As command overlord, jeftrk byf quickly assessed the situation and began to take charge. After coming in system, he was pleased to see the ship heading his way. After a quick calculation of its course and speed, his underlord had determined its most likely exit point. They had come out of light speed at a perfect angle to prevent them from reaching it. He had ordered the other overlords to take up chase positions to limit the evasive action the other ship could take. To his surprise, the ship just continued on course despite being clearly outmaneuvered at the moment. This made him a little nervous.

Returning to his command chair, he ordered the communication overling to open a channel to the bfnor torrnt. Once the connection was made, he said, "Overlord synska byf, this is Overlord jeftrk byf. What is your status?"

Synska byf was surprised to hear the voice of jeftrk byf. He would never have guessed he would have been selected to lead these ships. He answered, "We have taken a lot of damage trying to stop that ship Overlord. Out power relay is on backup, we have severe hull damage, and our speed has been reduced by one-third. We were breaking off when you arrived. I offer you whatever support the bfnor torrnt can provide."

Jeftrk byf knew the bfnor torrnt was a tough little ship. They must have taken a beating to suffer a hull breach. This information generated more concern. "What kind of capability have you witnessed with this ship so far?"

"They have deflective type shielding and a very powerful weapon. There is a turret on top that fires some kind of high-energy projectiles. They move at a surprising speed and carry a very heavy punch. Three projectiles blew through our outer and inner hulls. They don't seem to have deep penetration power, but they can cause severe damage to whatever they hit. I recommend extreme caution in dealing with them, Overlord," synska byf responded.

"Your concern is noted, Overlord. Update me on why they fired on you?"

"When I discovered the bfnor torrnt did not have the speed to overtake them, I fired a proximity mine in an attempt to slow them down. They were able to target and destroy the mine. They then fired back at us with the three bursts I mentioned earlier. We were completely disabled. Interesting thing though, Overlord, instead of finishing us off they appeared to return to our position to stop our drift. At first, I thought they were going to board us, but I have my doubts about that now. They left about the same time our power was restored. I can not say for sure if this was a contributing factor to their departure. One other thing to note, even though we fired at them again with two more mines, they did not return fire. They maneuvered away from the mines and then returned to the course you see now. That is when I broke off." Synska byf was hoping that the overlord would be able to take the lessons he learned and use it to his advantage.

"Thank you, Overlord, that will be all for now." Jeftrk byf signaled to the overling to break off the open channel. He was more confused now than before he talked with the overlord. It made sense that they would fire on the minelayer after it fired first. But then to return when they could have fled, just to stop them from drifting did not make sense to him. Could the overlord have been mistaken and they had meant to board the ship after all? Then again, why did they not fire back when the minelayer fired the second time? It made him wonder if this ship had detected their arrival, even though they were in light speed. "Could they have detected us coming in and started heading away?"

he said softly. But, if that was the case, wouldn't they have chosen a course that did not intersect with us? He looked at the ship again and wondered why it was choosing to continue on the intercept course. Could they have determined that his ships were not a threat to them? If they were basing that on what the minelayer was capable of doing, they were in for an unpleasant surprise. He had some nice ship stoppers on board these five ships. The other advantage he now had was the comment the overlord made about this ship maneuvering away from the mines. They would not have that luxury with his weapons. By the time they figured that out, it would likely be too late for them. He hoped anyway. He looked at the other ship again. "Just keep coming closer," he said to no one in particular.

This being the first encounter for the krracts, none of the overlords had any actual combat experience in their own war ships. This weighed heavily in the back of jeftrk byf's mind. He had been involved in attack simulation drills in the past, but they were mostly designed for defensive positioning from incoming ships. He was using one of these maneuvers in this situation. He was trying to box in the ship using a divide and destroy strategy. This was designed to separate ships from a fleet and quickly eliminate them through overwhelming firepower. He had separated his ships into the standard box format where he could reduce the ship's maneuvering room, thereby dictating where it could go. He was in the perfect scenario of having his prey cornered and outnumbered. In his mind, he felt that if it came to disabling the ship, he had the overwhelming firepower they had drilled for. The other commander must have understood this. He decided it was time to take the next step. He would be cautious though. Whoever was commanding that other ship appeared tricky.

Jeftrk byf ordered the leading ship, njyfur iguunc, to fire a warning shot across their path. When the fleeing ship did not react to the shot, he was even more puzzled. He watched as it continued to maintain its current course and speed. He was going to wait a few beats to give them time to think about the consequences. He looked over at his tracking overling who was reporting, "I am tracking a energy burst. It is heading towards the njyfur lguunc."

Looking up at the main viewer, jeftrk byf watched the tracking display as the fast moving burst crossed in front of the destroyer and continued towards his ship. The path of the burst and his ship were fast intersecting. Just as he was thinking about taking evasive action, the tracking image of the burst started to fade. Still quite a distance from his ship, the burst faded out altogether. He knew this had to be a warning shot because it had passed a good distant in front of the njyfur lguunc and well short of his ship.

"This has gone on long enough," jeftrk byf said. "It is time to stop playing a chasing game and make this ship stop." He intended to disable the ship and bring it back for research as he was ordered to do. This alien ship contained technology superior to his own and would be valuable to the Council. Bringing this ship back could even earn him a sli title. He would not pass up this opportunity. He was feeling the excitement of the hunt now. He would pit his intelligence and cunning against this newfound foe. Technology or not, he still felt he had the numbers on them. He was also pleased he did not have to worry about trying to split up its firepower. According to the overlord synsk byf, the only weapon it seemed to have was the top turret. This meant that they would only be able to attack one ship at a time, which was the perfect practice scenario he had trained for.

"Order the lead ships to open fire using primary weapons only. Have the kaffnur dneui target the gun emplacement. The njyfur lguunc is to target the high-energy signatures below the gun. Have the tuilmf target the exhaust ports. They are to commence firing at once," jeftrk byf ordered, then waited for the results. The lead ship, kaffnur dneui, having a clearer view, was feeding its image back to their view screen. He only half heard his orders being relayed.

The view screen showed all three ships as they fired. Jeftrk byf could see that they were right on target. The kaffnur dneui was firing at the top turret, but the energy beam was deflecting up and away from the ship. The other destroyer was not doing any better as the energy bolts were passing above and below the ship as they tried varying angles. The trailing destroyer was not getting through either, but the overlord noticed that shielding did not seem to deflect the shots as sharply as the others. He was trying to determine if this was an illusion from this angle or if a real weakness was being detected with their shielding. If it was a weakness, could he exploit it? He would have to give that some more thought later. He had other weapons that may prove more effective, at the moment.

He said, "Underlord, have all three lead ships switch weapons to missiles. They are to use the same target pattern. Have them fire as soon as they are ready."

The Privateer's deflector shielding was created by a series of emitters that protruded from overlapping points throughout the hull. Each emitter was tuned to project a magnetic deflection field to a specific depth from the ship's hull. The front emitters projected out thirty meters while the next inner set projected out twenty-nine meters and so on to create an arrow-shaped pattern. The side emitters projected out farthest from the center of the ship and narrowed as each emitter got closer to the top and bottom of the ship. The exhaust ports hampered the rear deflectors because of interference from the propulsion exhaust. The rear emitters had to be angled to project a flatter pattern that attempted to overlap where the exhaust emissions wreaked the most havoc.

On the bridge of the Privateer, Linda and Sharon watched as the three closest ships opened fire. The energy beams from each attacking ship was not able to penetrate the deflectors. Linda ordered that power to the rear emitters be increased while decreasing power to the port side emitters. She would have to reconsider the deflector power output if they had to veer to port. But, for now, she was glad she could steal a little power from that side. Protecting the ass end of the ship was her top priority.

Opening up a comm link, Linda ordered, "Commander Launtra, this is the captain. You may return fire. Disable A1 and then target A3. Once both vessels are neutralized, you may concentrate fire on A2."

Linda then commented to Sharon, "It is important that we protect our rear deflectors without appearing to do so. Targeting that closest ship first will hopefully give them the impression that we are selecting targets by how close they are to us. We can not afford to have our rear deflectors damaged should we have to turn away from those two larger bastards."

Sharon nodded while replying, "Targeting shows that the two larger ships will be in range in about four minutes. We are twenty-three minutes from reaching the safest point to launch, if we want to make a short emergency jump out of this system. If we can slow down that smaller lead ship, we may be able to warp out before the larger ones get close enough to bother us. Sensors show the ships have ceased fire. All emitters functioning to full capacity. The aft emitters functioning at three percent over capacity."

Bill was already targeting A1 when the captain ordered him to return fire. He had the other two ships locked into the targeting computer so that they could quickly receive a firing solution on each in turn. Knowing that the first ship was able to survive a three-bolt barrage, he decided on hitting these with four. The extra bolt might be enough to stop them longer than the first ship. He had a specialist enter a double burst discharge. Bill was also concerned about shielding. They couldn't detect any energy readings, but since these ships were alien it was always possible they were using something they couldn't detect.

The two guns belched out four highly charged plasma bolts with blinding speed. Bill quickly ordered the switch to A3. By the time he had selected the second target and the computer had swung the turret into place, the capacitors were fully charged. Again, the guns fired a four-bolt spread directly into the oncoming ship.

Before Bill had time to fire at the second ship, the first bolt struck the first ship eight meters aft of the bow, causing the ship to buck to the right slightly. The second bolt struck almost directly amidships, pushing the ship farther to the right of its original course. The third bolt hit aft of amidships, causing the now powerless ship to spin to the left. The final bolt stuck the swinging ship just slightly aft of the bow, nearly stopping its momentum. The doomed ship was slowing spinning and drifting in space. Bill, not having time to view his first shots, was now watching the track of his second shot sequence. All four bolts struck the smaller ship head on. The first bolt had eliminated the bow section, leaving a gaping hole. The second bolt traveled into the open bow and struck the next intact bulkhead. The ship disintegrated. The third and fourth bolts followed right in after the first two, each one adding to the boiling mass that now represented the destroyed ship.

The quickness of the bolts had caused Bill to watch the results of his second series of shots to gauge the results. He could not believe the damage he had just inflicted on that ship. He quickly shifted view to the first target ship and watched in amazement as it slowly spun. The displayed view was showing the right front bow section all but gone, while the midsection displayed a large round hole. There was a similar hole near the aft section. It took a moment for Bill to return focus to his tasks. He finally remembered to switch to the final target. A2 had turned and was attempting to flee. Bill thought about holding off firing, but he had not received orders to do so. Once the targeting computer locked onto the target and had set the turret to the proper firing angle, it was just a matter of pressing the firing button. Bill had the shot sequence reduced to a single spread. He had overestimated the structural stability of these alien vessels. Bill now realized that they were not able to withstand the abuse that the first ship they encountered had.

The loss of two of the krracts war ships shocked synska byf. He now observed the fleeing kaffnur dneui. The remaining destroyer was straining to put distance between the two ships. He could just make out the two bright dots that could only be from the alien ship's weapon. He watched in silence as the desperate overlord tried to turn away from the incoming shots. The bright dots had the ship's angle. He could see that they were going to strike the ship regardless of what the overlord did. The destroyer was making a wild reverse of direction, but it was the last act of a desperate overlord. Synska byf watched in horror as each shot struck the ship. Even at their current distance from the destroyer, he could tell that each bolt had vaporized large sections of the hull. He shook his head in disbelief. He had warned them of the damaging firepower of that ship. This was going to prove to be a very costly lesson for them all.

The destroyer was now drifting. As it slowly spun around, synska byf could see that the hull had been breached just aft of the main propulsion compartment. The hull was still venting the life out of the exposed section. He was not surprised to see the damage inflicted, having experienced the firepower himself. He felt sorry for the other overlords who were now getting their own lesson.

"Underlord, change course to take us alongside the kaffnur dneui. We may be able to render aid," synska byf ordered. The thought of his own helplessness from the same kind of damage was still fresh in his mind. While his ship had the double hull construction, these older destroyers contained just a single hull. Being older, they did not have the shielding the larger cruisers had. He was looking at the results of that now. He knew the Council would have to rethink the future of this aging fleet, especially if they encountered more of these dangerous ships.

"As you wish, Overlord," brk'erst responded. He was also shocked at the ease at which three of their fighting vessels were eliminated. He was feeling fortunate that they were still alive.

Aboard the ghontuf, jeftrk byf watched in disbelief as his lead destroyer went dead in space and the tuilmf seemed to just disappear. He was now concentrating on the third destroyer as it turned away from the deadly ship. He nodded as he was informed that the alien ship had just fired another salvo of those deadly balls of light. He knew that he was powerless to help. In less than three beats, the destroyer was hit twice. It was now spinning as it drifted along out of control. He nodded again when the underlord notified him that the bfnor torrnt had altered course toward the stricken destroyer. Glancing over at the tracking display, he noted the range between his two cruisers and the alien ship. They were just reaching maximum range for the missiles they carried. Between the two remaining ships, they could fire sixteen per salvo. Heat–activated, these deadly weapons would follow their prey until they struck it. It is hard to hide your heat in the cold of space, he thought, as he looked on at the other ship.

Jeftrk byf thought to himself, if I was on that ship and sixteen missiles were fired at me, what would I do? At this distance, I would most likely turn away and try to outrun them. He knew that if the other ship turned away they would easily outdistance the missiles. "We must get closer to prevent them from being able to run beyond the range of my missiles," he said to no one in particular. The overlord made up his mind that he would wait until they were well within range. He wondered if the new shielding of his ship could withstand the power of that alien ship's weapon. Looking at the two remaining destroyers, he was wondering why the bfnor torrnt was still in one piece. It was apparent that this ship had the capability to blow a helpless minelayer into particles.

Another thought came to jeftrk byf. His first two ships had been hit with four shots each while the last one was hit with only two. He wondered if this was a limitation of their weapon's system or a change in strategy. If it was a change, he wondered why they would have done that. Were they concerned about the damage they had done to the first two ships? If so, why would they care? "What is your game," he said softly. He wanted to disable that other ship if for no other reason than to meet this most intriguing creature. Whoever was in control was a very capable, if not confusing, foe. He sat down in the command chair to think this whole thing over in his mind. There must be some way that I can use what I have just learned, he thought. Well, time was still on his side for the moment. His only hope was that the ship would stay on its current course. He needed to close the gap, and they were helping him do it.

The sensor arrays were looking over the two damaged ships. Both were displaying minimal power output. It was apparent neither ship had any major power capacity. Both ships were still venting through their damaged hull, which was a sure sign that the damage was more sever than what they had witnessed with the first ship they encountered. Linda wondered if any damage control was going on in those ships. The last ship they had hit was spinning badly, which would make damage control difficult for that crew. Unless the internal stabilizers were countering the spin, the crew would be hard pressed to stay oriented. Linda turned her focus on the two remaining ships still attempting to cut off her escape. She ordered a course change to head for the second jump point. This would put the Privateer on an angle trailing slightly away from the two remaining ships, thereby reducing their ability to fire on her ship. She was not as concerned with the rear deflectors since the faster ships were out of action. She was sure these ships were not in range yet to fire their energy weapons. She was also confident that she could outmaneuver those missile type devices they fired. She felt bad about that little vessel they blew apart, but she knew it was an act of survival now. She felt relieved knowing that the two undamaged ships could not outpace the Privateer in speed. She only needed the Privateer to keep moving to get out of this situation.

Linda sat heavily into her chair. She realized that she was tired and hungry. The adrenaline racing through her as she ordered the firing on the three ships, was now wearing off. If she was tired it was a good bet the rest of the crew was, too. She had Sharon take charge of getting some cold sandwiches made up and given to the crew. She knew Sharon would insure that this included drinks as well. Once they reached warp, she would have the crew stand down and return to regular duty. Looking at the images of the damaged ships, disappearing into the distance, she knew there would be a day of reckoning for all that happened here. She wondered if anyone could kill that many people, alien or not, and not have to atone for it later. The thought starting to depress her, so she shook it off to focus on the problems at hand.

Activating the comm unit, she selected all circuits and said, "This is the captain. The Privateer was fired on by three of the five ships pursuing us. I ordered the return fire on these three ships and they are all, now, out of action. The Privateer is now angling away from the other two and should reach the jump point without further trouble." With this said she shut down the comm unit and tried to relax.

"The target ship has altered course, Overlord." This made jeftrk byf swear loudly as he watched the ship veer away from him. They had gained a good chunk of distance over the past three hundred beats, but not enough to make his missiles truly effective. He thought that if luck was with him today, he may get a missile or two through.

"Underlord, coordinate with the piirfh njyfn and fire a full spread of missiles," he ordered. Once the missiles were away, he would have the piirfh njyfn alter course to come alongside the damaged destroyer to provide assistance. He would continue to pursue with the slim hope that something might happen that would allow him to catch this most intriguing species.

Sharon had made her way down to the mess hall to get the cooks to quickly make up a bunch of sandwiches for the crew. As a stack of sandwiches were made up, she would have a steward run them over to various departments. She was a little annoyed of having to do this kind of work. It shouldn't take an exec to supervisor feeding the crew, she thought. Sharon had decided that her talents were wasted on the boring, tedious work aboard the setup ships. Especially one such as the Privateer. She didn't see herself running between assignment and the station, doing the same work over and over. Nope, this is not for me, she decided. I am so gone when this tub gets back to Rap. I am going to get me a fat tanker or freighter with the guild. A rumble over her head brought Sharon out of her thoughts. Realizing what the noise was from, she grabbed a platter full of sandwiches and headed out.

When the word came in that the last two ships had fired, Linda popped out of her chair. Tracking was recording the flight of sixteen inbound objects. The specialist also noted that they were not of the same design as those they had dealt with before. These were proving to be much faster. Sharon had not returned to the bridge yet, requiring Linda to insure her orders were being carried out correctly. "Hard to starboard," she ordered.

The Privateer pulled hard to the right. Linda counted to ten and then ordered hard to Port. She counted to five and ordered the Privateer back on its original course. She asked the tracking specialist if the incoming weapons had been affected by the maneuver. She was told that each weapon had altered right slightly on her starboard turn and then adjusted back again as the Privateer returned to her original course. It was apparent that these weapons were able to lock onto her ship and adjust to follow it. She wondered if they were using heat or mass to lock on. Since she didn't know the range of these weapons, her only hope now was to try to pick off as many of the incoming missiles as they could, then try to outmaneuver the rest. She ordered Bill to track and pick off as many of the missiles as possible. She knew he could not get all of them. If he could pick off half, they would be doing well. She also told him to start with the leftmost missiles and work his way down the line. She was hoping that this would help her in working a starboard turn angle without giving up much distance to the jump point. She nodded when she was informed that A5 had altered course and was heading back toward A1. Good, one down one to go, she thought to herself.

She then paused to ponder why the second large ship had veered off. There would only be two reasons, the way she saw it. Either they expected these missiles to finish her off where only one ship was needed for mop-up, or they were firing at a range that provided little hope for success. But which was it? Guessing wrong could prove fatal. She decided to just stay the course and hope for the best. She watched the status screen to see how Bill was doing in trying to destroy the missiles.

Back in the weapons area, Bill worked with the specialists as they began selecting targets for the computer tracking system. They were going to try to mark four at a time. Bill thought they might get about ten of them if they could prevent delays in tracking. He had Trium and Mila working the targeting computer while he stayed on tracking. Don would handle the firing. The two remaining ships were now within firing range, but he did not have time to worry about that yet. He would give them something to think about before they could fire again, he promised himself. Bill watched as the first four targets went red. Don pressed the fire button and waited for the computer-controlled guns to respond. Each barrel was set for a single shot. Two shots per missile would allow for quicker recharging. When the first two shots went out, Bill counted to five and had Don fire again. He listened to the next two reports from the guns. He continued this through all four targets.

"Done, target the next four. Look alive, folks. Our lives are at stake here," he ordered.

Don looked up and said, "The target missiles five and six have altered course toward the last set of bolts you fired."

Bill altered his view from the targeting computer to the tracking display. Sure enough, two of the next four missiles were now tracking plasma bolts. "It must be the heat they're emitting," he said. Smiling, he decided to change tactics.

"Change turret and gun control from computer to manual," he ordered as he switched on the turret scope. Using manual controls, he swung the turret guns so they were aimed slightly left of the rightmost missile and well above it. He then fired the guns to send out two plasma bolts, knowing the bolts would strike each other where they converged. He knew that when the two bolts exploded the heat signature would be large. Hopefully, large enough to draw the missiles towards it.

Bill kept his focus on the two bolts he had fired, even when tracking was recording the impact of the earlier computer-controlled shots. He needed to gauge the effect this strategy would have while also allowing the capacitors to recharge. He looked away from the scope when the bolts met and exploded. Three more blasts in quick succession followed the explosion.

It took several seconds for the explosions to die away enough for tracking to pick up the missiles again. All but two had turned toward the explosion. A quick count showed that the rightmost three missiles were gone. As expected, they followed right into the mix of the plasma burst and exploded. The original four left missiles he had targeted were also gone, as were the two that had turned to track the incoming bolts. Nine of sixteen missiles were gone. Five missiles were just now turning away from the explosion and heading onwards towards the ship. They had lost ground in the maneuver and were back of the remaining two. Bill fired two more bolts directly in the path of the set of five missiles. He then had his specialists set up a track on the remaining two missiles. He had the turret and gun control returned to the computer.

Once again, the targeting computer was used to lock onto the last two missiles. They were setting up for a two-shot burst at each missile as before. The tracking computer recorded the blast of the two manually fired bolts he had shot just a moment ago. Bill decided he would look into that when he had destroyed these two. A target lock signal was received, and Don fired. When the second target lock was received, he fire again.

Rushing through the routine to fire at the last two missiles, Bill had made a critical error. He had tracked and fired at the left missile first, followed by a shot at the right missile. This mistake had caused the first bolts to pass in front of the right missile as they continued on to the left. Sensing the heat, the right missile had altered course to pursue the plasma bolts. Because of the speed of the bolts, the missile could not respond fast enough to keep the bolts within its heat sensor. The missile lost the heat signature of the bolts, but regained the signature of the ship. The missile swung back onto its original target. This sudden change of direction allowed the second set of bolts to pass harmlessly behind the missile.

Bill had returned to manual tracking and had swung the turret back toward the final five missiles to see what remained. He knew that the tracking computer would be unusable until it settled back down after all the plasma bursts and missile explosions. In the turret scope, Bill could see that four of the five missiles were gone. He quickly lined up the turret and fired a final burst directly at that last remaining missile. He sat back and watched the two plasma bolts take the missile out. He sighed and spun the scope away from him.

The tracking computer slowly began to come back to life as the interference died down. The two large ships came in first, followed closely by the drifting smaller ships. Finally, the last remaining missile came in. Don jerked back and yelled out that they had contact on another missile. He yelled out coordinates while Trium and Mila tried to get it locked into the targeting computer. Bill had the turret returned to computer control. He looked at both the tracking and targeting displays and knew they could not get a lock and fire in time to stop this one. The turret guns could not be angled down on the target. He knew that there was not enough time to coordinate getting the bridge to lean the ship over to the right.

Bill switched on his comm unit and said, "Bridge, weapons, one missile has gotten though. We can't stop it. Brace for impact!"

Not bothering to answer Bill, Linda said, "Sound the collision alarm. Brace for impact." She then looked at the missiles incoming angle and quickly realized that the missile appeared to be heading towards the turret. She guessed that the weapon was tracking heat, as the gun barrels would be extremely hot after firing all those bolts. She determined that this was probably the best place and angle to take the hit. Although it would probably jam the turret, there was little other risk to the ship's critical functions. She decided not the attempt to alter course. She was just preparing to tell Bill to abandon the compartment when the missile struck.

The missile ran out of fuel just shy of its target. This sudden loss of propulsion thrust allowed the Privateer to pull ahead of the missile slightly. Unfortunately for the crew of the Privateer this allowed the missile to strike just aft of the gun turret as the missile drifted off its intended strike point.

Damage to the starboard side emitters, from where the two mines had exploded earlier, left a slight gap in the overlap below and aft of the gun turret. The section where the missile struck the deflector shielding was at a point where these two emitters should have overlapped. The emitter closest to the missile was not projecting out far enough. This produced a slight gap between it and the next emitter. The missiles explosive power blew through the open gap and against the ship's hull. Once inside the shielding, the blow back off the hull bounced off the shielding and was forced back against the hull again.

Sharon was taking a shortcut through the crew's quarters in order to get to the emergency control room faster. It was the closest compartment from the mess hall, where she could get information as to what was going on. When she had heard the turret swinging around from the mess hall, she had a sense of urgency to get back on station. When the guns started firing, she was trying to get there as fast as she could. The wild maneuvers of the ship were not helping her any, she thought. Suddenly, she was thrown clean off her feet. The platter in her hands bounced off the ceiling and clattered to the decking. Sharon never heard it; she had hit the bulkhead on the opposite side so hard, she was out cold.

Bill was standing when the missile struck. Even though he had a firm grip on an overhead support rail, the blast tossed him across the compartment and into a bulkhead. His specialists were thrown out of their chairs and onto the floor. One of the main conduits to the turret sheared away from the ceiling, as the entire floor seemed to buckle upwards. Emergency controls detected the uncontrolled release of plasma and routed the plasma discharge through the emergency vents and away from the conduits. The computer also shut down the main firing generators to prevent them from trying to recharge the capacitors. This rapid reroute of plasma discharge saved the lives of all those in the weapons control room.

In the engine room, the explosion rocked the propulsion system. The shock absorbing mounts were rocked beyond their limits. The shock-control computer detected the strain on the mounts, causing it to shut down the propulsion system to guard against damage. Throughout the ship, the steady hum of the main engines slowly died away.

In emergency control, Rebecca tried to make sense of the multitude of warning lights that were being displayed by the backup computer system. She tried contacting the bridge, but she could not get an answer. She correctly assumed that the communication system was down. The navigational display was out, so she couldn't take over guidance if she needed to. She could tell from both feel and warning displays that the main propulsion units were shutting down. With the emergency control room being just forward of the engine room, she decided to take the risk of leaving the control room to see what was happening in engineering. She left orders for a specialist to notify her the moment that communication was restored.

Up on the bridge, Linda came to her feet with the help of a specialist. She had twisted her ankle when she was thrown off her feet. It was throbbing as she tried to put weight on it. She hobbled to her chair and sat down. She ignored the pain and looked around the bridge. Most of the displays that had gone out in their earlier battle were out again. She wanted to contact emergency control, but her comm unit was dangling alongside her chair. It was slowing swinging on a few frayed wires. She must have grabbed onto it when she was tossed about, she determined. She looked over at the communication station and could see the entire board was dark. She yelled out to get communication back on line. Specialists raced over and started removing access panels to get to the vitals within. She was confident that they would have it up and running soon. She wondered how long it would take that other ship to reload its missile banks. She figured they had that long to get back in control of the ship.

Bill found himself sitting with his back to a bulkhead. His right arm was numb, preventing him from using it. He thought he must have hit the bulkhead pretty hard. Leaning on his left arm, he came to his knees. Seeing the cloud of heated plasma that still hung around the ceiling, he knew he had to stay low. He yelled out for everyone else to do the same. Even though he could hear the plasma being routed through the emergency venting system, he could still see small amounts escaping the damaged conduits in small puffs. One good thing about his being thrown over to the bulkhead was that he was within reach of the emergency breathing devices. He reached up and grabbed one. He had to hold it between his knees so he could twist the knob to start the oxygen flow. His right arm was still numb, but he could tell that feeling was beginning to return. He put the mask to his face and took several deep breaths before setting it down again. With only the one arm, he knew he would waste too much time fighting to get it on his head. While holding his breath, he started grabbing and throwing the rest to each specialist, then ordered the space to be evacuated. He picked up the breathing device and held it to his face as he raced for the hatch. Insuring everyone was out, he ordered the hatch closed and sealed.

Deciding that the bridge was his next logical step, Bill decided to head that way. Before he left, he ordered his specialists to head for the mess hall to wait for further orders. He instructed them not to remove their breathing devices until they were out of this passageway. He took a couple more deep draws off the device to help clear his lungs before throwing it aside. He headed in the opposite direction to reach the bridge. He used the main passageway to reach the emergency ladder. He was hoping to avoid having to rely on the lifts. Reaching the bridge, Bill stopped to catch his breath. Linda looked relieved to see him. Bill provided her with a quick summary of the damage to the weapons station. Linda ordered him to head for emergency control and take over the ship until they could get the bridge up and running again. He stopped when Linda yelled, "Wait!" She pulled out a set of single frequency communicators and threw one to him, yelling, "Go!" as soon as he caught it.

Bill raced into the emergency control room completely exhausted. Out of breath, he was unable to talk. His arm had lost most of its numbness, though it was throbbing. He started looking over each display panel and began overriding bridge controls. He was about to asked where Rebecca was when she returned from the engine room and said, "The engineering specialists were overriding the safety controls and should have the propulsion system back up shortly. They were concerned about attempting to restart them while they were so hot, but I told them that if we stayed here and waited for those other ships to catch up, it would get much hotter. I think I impressed upon them the need to bypass some safety measures."

"Good thinking, Rebecca," Bill commented.

Seeing no need for the both of them in the emergency control room, Bill had Rebecca return to the engine room to see if she could help speed things along. Bill sat down heavily and caught his breath. His scamper through the ship had left him hot and sweaty. He was thankful for the few moments of quiet. He could feel the vibration as the propulsion units started to come back on line. He rolled his chair over to a terminal and got ready for the full return of mobility.

Looking over the various displays, Bill could see that the navigational unit was the only emergency backup system not running at the moment. Bill used the tracking computer to validate their current heading. He decided they would stay on this course until one of the navigation computers came on line. He had one of the specialists begin working on their navigation computer to see if it could be repaired quickly. Bill could now hear the powerful propulsion system as they increased their power output. The ship lurched forward a couple of times before smoothing out. He knew that time had run out for them. The weapons system was out for good, so it was now an all out race to reach warp. The tracking computer was still showing one of the larger ships in pursuit, but no more missiles had been fired.

Bill activated his handheld comm unit and said, "Captain?"

"Talk to me, Bill," she answered quickly.

"We have control of the ship. Engines are back on line, and we should be back to full speed in a few minutes. All systems are operational with the exception of navigation. We are working on it now. I am using the tracking computer to keep us moving along our current course. I will not be able to jump to warp without navigational support. I still show one ship tracking us, and they have made up considerable distance. We will continue to monitor them for any activity. Ship maneuvering will be slow using tracking only, but it is better than none at all. Hopefully, we will have navigation controls back before they can fire again," Bill reported.

Linda responded, "We should only be a few minutes away from the jump point now. If we get our navigation system working first, we will feed the coordinates in so you can make a short jump. We will keep our fingers crossed up here. Do the best you can until we can resume control. Let's pray that it takes a while for them to reload a missile." She then told the specialists to forget the communication station and get navigation up first. She watched as one of the specialists left the communication station and started pulling the panels from the navigation console.

Something was bothering Linda but she couldn't seem to put her finger on it. She looked around the bridge when it came to her that Sharon was still missing. Her first instincts would have been to either come to the bridge or emergency control, whichever was closer, to get up to speed and receive further orders from Linda. Activating the handheld unit she asked, "Bill, did you run into Sharon at all?"

"No Captain, I did not see her at all. Do you need me to see if I can track her down? She may have run into a damaged area and taken control of getting it fixed," Bill replied

Thinking for a few moments, Linda tried to decide what this meant. As much of a pain as Sharon was, she would never had abandoned her duties. She finally responded to Bill, "No Bill, stay where you are. I am sure she will show up once she frees up from what she is going."

※ ※ ※

Jeftrk byf watched as groups of his missiles were taken out. The ghontuf was now only showing seven of them, and five were chasing after a ghost explosion. These were very clever beings on that ship, he determined. The piirfh njyfn had broken off and was fast approaching the disabled njyfur Iguunc. He watched as another series of bolts fired from that most impressive weapon. They were aiming at the set of missiles that had remained on target. He observed the explosion, and one of the missiles disappeared from the display. Of the five in the other set, another four disappeared in the wake of fire. They were tracking two single missiles now, and one of them was at its extreme range. He knew it had to be nearly out of fuel. He then watched as another missile was eliminated. He was thinking what a wonderful weapon they had and how much he would like to get his hands on it.

He was just about to give up hope when an overling reported that a missile had hit on target. He looked at the tracking display, which validated that the computer was reporting a missile strike near mid-section. Could this be the break he was hoping for? The overling reported again that the target ship was slowing and venting was being detected out the top of the ship just aft of the gun. "Yes!" the overlord shouted.

Jeftrk byf was leaning forward in his chair in an unconscious effort to speed his ship along. They were closing the distance rapidly now as the other ship glided along without propulsion. He looked at his underlord and asked, "Where are we at on reloading another missile, underlord?"

The underlord responded that two tubes would be reloaded in about thirteen beats. Jeftrk byf could see that the tables were turning on these most formidable creatures. In a moment, he was going to have two missiles at his disposal. He intended to fire both, knowing they would track and strike at the heated exhaust ports. He noted the venting out the top of the ship. He was pretty sure that this was related to that weapon of theirs. He now suspected the weapon was out of action. He smiled as he said, "You led a good chase, my prey, but you will be mine and nothing is going to prevent that now."

He wished he could tell if the shielding was still up. They were not close enough yet to use the energy beam. When he got within range, he would fire a short burst to see if it got through. Without that protection, he would target the gun emplacement to insure it stayed out of action. He ordered the course heading to fall off a bit to put his ship directly behind the other. He hoped this would help to guide the missiles directly up the exhaust ports. He could see the heat signature on the tracking display. He sat back and waited for the two missiles to be loaded. He knew that they could only load two at a time without causing his underlings to fall all over themselves. He ordered, "Underlord, make every effort to speed along the loading. I want that ship, and I will have it. It we wait too long the exhaust ports will cool off, causing our missiles to have a hard time finding a heat source. "

The tracking overling reported that the ship was accelerating again. Slowly but surely, they were picking up speed. They were still venting out the top. Jeftrk byf looked at the underlord, who only shook his head. The underlord knew that his command overlord was interested in the status of the missiles.

"Fire each of the missiles as soon as they become ready. You do not need to wait for my order on this. I will be most displeased if we lose this opportunity because of an inefficient crew," commented jeftrk byf. He then smiled when the underlord said that they were within range of the main weapon.

"Set for full intensity. Fire at the exhaust ports," ordered jeftrk byf. He decided to focus on the ports first in an effort to knock out propulsion again. Once he had accomplished that, he would have them switch to the gun emplacement. The fact that the other ship had not returned fire confirmed they had lost their ability to use it. At least he hoped that was the case.

A stream of light shot out from his ship and raced on to strike the aft end of the other ship. The beam bent slightly as it neared the ship. The tracking display was showing some of the beam was passing through. The overlord smiled to himself as he watched another burst shoot away toward the fleeing ship.

The Privateer had reached the calculated launch point and was streaking past it. Neither navigational computer was on line yet. The computer refused to boot up in emergency control, leading Bill to believe it was hopelessly damaged by the impact of the explosion. The news from the bridge was that the navigation programming to the main computer was initializing, but it had not reached the point of control yet. They would then need a few more minutes to reload the jump point coordinates to obtain the navigational fix. This was assuming the software would respond once the unit was back up again.

The good news was that the bridge had tracking back on line and took over the responsibility of watching their pursuer. Propulsion was another matter because the main drive engines were overheating again. There was a problem with the cooling system, but, so far, the engineering specialists could not find it. If they went into warp with a cooling problem on the mains, they risked blowing apart in a matter of minutes. The only clue they had was that the coolant pressure coming into the engine room was down nearly forty percent.

The Privateer shook slightly as the first burst of an energy beam struck the rear shield. Some of the beam passed through to strike harmlessly against the exhaust housing. The beam had been weakened by its passage through the deflector shielding and the ion emissions. The ship shook again as another burst hit them. Bill thought about altering course slightly, but decided it would only delay getting the navigational numbers calculated. Their only hope was in the bridge navigational unit coming on line soon.

On the bridge, Linda cringed every time the Privateer shook. She knew that it was only a matter of time before one of the beams broke through directly over an exhaust port. An energy burst directly into the exhaust port could cause enough back pressure to stall the propulsion system, or worse, back-blast into engineering. She was silently saying a prayer in the hope that they would get into warp before that happened.

A tracking overling was reporting that the alien ship was showing a slight decrease in forward thrust. Jeftrk byf wondered if their firing was having an effect on their propulsion. It appeared they were at a point where they could jump. He felt the recoil of the ship as a missile launched, then another. The overlord snapped his jaws at the fleeing ship. Their time had run out. They had led a good chase, but he had their scent; they wouldn't get away from him now. The underlord informed him that two more missiles were being loaded. If both missiles struck that ship from behind, he was sure it would stop them dead in their tracks. He was even hopeful it would drop the shielding as well. Then, he would disable the turret gun for sure. That should soften them up enough to keep them docile for the trip back to the Council, he thought. He would return a hero like no overlord before him.

"As soon as the two missiles strike the shielding, inform me of the results. Keep the primary weapons targeting the shielding. Let's see if we can continue to slow them down and give our missiles a smaller travel distance. If their shields drop, concentrate on disabling the gun," jeftrk byf ordered.

Linda reported to Bill that two more missiles had been detected. They could not risk increasing speed for fear of hastening the overheating of the propulsion system. Rebecca had told Bill that they had bypassed the emergency control module to prevent the engines from shutting down automatically. The starboard side deflectors were out again, only this time there would be no hope in fixing them. The explosion had damaged the deflector emitters. There was no way to fix them from within the ship. It had come down to what would happen first: get the navigation computer working or take two hits on the weak rear deflectors. Linda was toying with the idea of altering course to put the port side deflectors toward the missiles, but she didn't want to have to turn away from the jump point. Their best option was to jump away from this mess and try to fix the ship enough to get home. She only hoped they couldn't track her once she made the leap into warp.

The overheating of the propulsion system was leaving a long trail of heated exhaust behind the ship, thereby providing the missiles with a strong signature. The missiles were moving directly along the Privateer's path. Although the aft shielding was weak, it still provided some measure of protection. Linda knew that even though the rear deflectors would absorb some of the explosion, she had no doubt that they would take damage back there. Hopefully, having the safety features overridden might keep the propulsion units on line. Another energy beam struck the rear deflectors, causing five emitters to fail. The damage control panel lights went red, showing where each failed emitter existed on the hull. They now had a large section of aft hull exposed as well as one of the exhaust ports.

Linda was startled when a cheer came from the specialists. They had the navigation computer up and running again. The race was on to get the navigational coordinates ready for a jump to warp. She didn't need to express the urgency in that order. Linda also notified Bill that they had navigational control and were entering the coordinates for the jump. She was thankful that the company had the foresight to provide backup communication devices, even one as simple as the two-way units she shared with Bill. Two of the specialists headed back to the communication console in an attempt to fix it as well.

Another beam struck the aft of the ship just left of the exhaust port. The metal hull turned red, then white, before exploding, leaving a sizable hole in the aft bulkhead. The hole exposed a compartment that provided service access to the exhaust port ducting. Fortunately for the engineering crew, no one was in this space at the time of the breach. Warning lights and sirens went off signifying the hull breach.

Tracking was reporting that the two missiles were just three thousands meters and closing fast. Linda provided the navigational calculations to the navigator who entered them into the system. As soon as the specialist repeated the numbers, Linda ordered the jump to warp. The crew, as the ship shot out of normal space, gladly felt the familiar forward pull. The first jump was only calculated for one minute, but it would put a world of distance between them and the trouble that followed.

Bill watched the propulsion status display for the main drive units. The cooling system was overheating at a much faster pace now. Whatever had bothered the cooling of the standard propulsion unit was also affecting the warp drive units. Bill did a quick calculation in his head to determine how long they could continue before they would have to drop out of warp again. He estimated that they could continue for no more than two minutes.

Jeftrk byf was elated when their sensor showed that the energy beam was penetrating through the shielding. Their next shot had clearly hit the hull, and venting could be seen coming from it. If they could only hit one of the exhaust ports, he thought. It was hard to pinpoint the beam at this distance, but they were causing damage now, so it was only a matter of time. He also watched as each missile neared the target. It was only a matter of a few beats more. The overlord could hardly contain his excitement. Suddenly the ship seemed to stretch like a piece of rubber, then disappeared completely. There was no doubting where they went. He had seen enough ships jump into light speed to recognize the effect it played on one's vision. In its wake, they left him with nothing but destruction. He decided it was time to gather up what was left of his small fleet and head for home. He had the energy beam focused on the missiles to prevent them from turning back on his own ship.

Retiring to his living space to replay the entire event, jeftrk byf could not help but be disappointed. He had lost the greatest opportunity of his life. Who knew if they would ever see another ship like that again? They may never return after this encounter, he thought. He now needed to transmit an update to the Council. The most difficult update he would ever have to give. Before he reported in, though, he was determined to go over everything that had happened since he'd arrived on scene. He would have to answer many questions upon his return. As he replayed the entire incident in his mind, he wondered what would have happened had he kept his destroyers closer to his cruisers. Maybe he should have had the destroyers fire a salvo of missiles first. Between the three destroyers, they could have fired ten at once. Coming in from different angles may have made it harder for the other ship to pick them off. Maybe he should have had the three ships open up with all weapons instead of just the energy beam. The overlord of the minelayer had warned him of the shielding that the ship possessed. He had no doubt that the Council members would focus on his tentative decision to use limited firepower from the start. But, he had only wanted to disable the ship so he could tow it back to the Council for their inspection. He doubted the Council members would care about his version of why he did not produce the ship.

The Privateer came out of warp exactly sixty seconds after entering it. The planets that had become so familiar to them during the ordeal were now just tiny dots in the sky. A quick scan showed the area was void of any other objects. For this, Linda was thankful. She ordered a constant scanner sweep as she retired to her office to send a final message before they returned to light speed again. She was already working the words over in her head as she sat behind her desk.

THE KRRACTS ENCOUNTER

ATD: 2353; Date: 2246; Priority AAAA; From: Captain Linda Eccles; Privateer; To: CEO Ernest T. Leander; and ADM Wilson Swensen; Message as follows:

Upon leaving, disabled alien vessel encountered fleet of five ships. Three light, two heavies. Angle of pursuit by incoming fleet of ships cut across jump point. Attempted to continue on course to leave system. The three lights split to take up positions aft and starboard of Privateer's course. Received warning shot from front leading light. Returned warning shot and maintained course. Received energy beam style fire from all three lights with no effect. Ordered weapons control to return fire to disable lights. Concentrated on closest vessel, followed by trailing vessel, and ending with starboard vessel. Results were one light destroyed and two out of action. Received responding fire from two heavies in the form of missiles. Sixteen were fired simultaneously with only one getting past defensive fire. Exploding single missile caused loss of key system and propulsion. Valiant effort by crew and coordination between emergency control and bridge allowed Privateer to continue her flight. Reached jump point just as second volley of two missiles was launched. Dropped out of warp after quick jump. Current position is 477.98113.006. Returning to warp and coming home upon completion of repairs to cooling system. Will exit warp at Orbiter-3 in twenty-three days, six hours. Time approximate based on time of receipt of this message along with time to repair. Will relay if repairs cause a delay in estimated arrival time. Recommend crew and officers of Privateer for medal of valor and extra pay associated with duty above and beyond. Respectfully, Linda Eccles, Captain, Privateer.

Communication had been restored shortly after the Privateer dropped out of warp. Bill moved to the bridge to take over for the captain. Bill sent Rebecca on a search for Sharon. Slowly, things were returning to normal.

"Captain, Bridge," Bill sent over the communication channel to the captain.

"Yes, Bill, what can I do for you?" Linda answered through the comm unit.

"Rebecca just reported in that Sharon has been located. She has been taken to sick bay for observation. She reported that Sharon had been passing through the corridor close to the missile impact area. She was thrown against the bulkhead and has a severe concussion. She is unconscious at the moment. The medic is keeping a close eye on her in case she shows any signs of brain swelling. The medic is deeply concerned about her Captain," Bill reported sadly.

"Meet me outside the weapons control room at once, Bill," Linda ordered.

Feeling extremely tired now, Linda met up with Bill to assess the damage to the weapons control room. She agreed with Bill's assessment that the plasma leak and conduit damage would have to wait for the ship repair yard at Rap-3. The seal around the compartment hatch was checked for leakage. When no leakage was found, Linda ordered the compartment locked down. Together they went on to sick bay to get an update on Sharon.

Sharon did not look good at all. She was very pale with a dark purple coloring around the right temple. Linda took one look and asked the medic, "What can you tell me about her condition, Steve?"

Steve was a general practitioner hired onto the Privateer for general medical needs and providing care for the occasional accidents. He knew that Sharon has suffered a very nasty blow to the head and was very concerned with possible brain injury from swelling. He responded, "I am very concerned about her, Captain. If there is swelling going on in there, I don't have the equipment on this ship to do anything about it. I could end up killing her, just trying to save her. All we can hope for right now is that she has a severe concussion and will be out for a day or two. If is it worse than that, we will be powerless to help her."

"Thanks, Steve. Do what you can for her and let me know the minute anything changes," Linda said. She looked around and noted the others who were also being cared for. Mostly it looked like broken bones and lacerations from being thrown around. She added, "I thank you all for your hard work in keeping the ship running during this troubling time. It hurts me deeply to see the injuries you received while just trying to do your duty. Keep your spirits up. You should be happy to know that your efforts have helped us get clear and now we will be heading for home. I am proud of you all."

Returning to the bridge, Linda ordered that a special meal be prepared for the crew with rotations set up to allow for all officers and crew to be fed. She then ordered that a skeleton crew be identified for running the Privateer to allow the crew to receive rest.

The engineers spent nearly an hour tracking down the cooling problem. The starboard cooling conduit had been badly crimped where it passed alongside the bulkhead between two compartments. The missile blast had caused the outer ship's hull to buckle into the conduit. The crimped conduit had caused a reduction in coolant flow to one of the propulsion units. The conduit had to be cut away enough to allow for access to the damaged hull. Large jackscrews were used to push the hull back out to provide clearance for a new section of conduit. Once the conduit was spliced and the seals tested, the Privateer was on her way again.

❈ ❈ ❈

The two krracts cruisers headed home, each towing a severely damage destroyer. The loss of life on each had been high. The bfnor torrnt stayed behind long enough to set up a series of buoys to more closely monitor the system. They also set all of their remaining mines along the entry and exit points of both the first object and the now departed ship. Lastly, they pick up the buoy they had launched for communicating with the Council. Once retrieved, they headed for home, limping along using the same route the cruisers had taken. After the long ordeal with the unknown ship, the overlord was thankful for the long, quiet trip back. He had gone aboard the destroyer kaffnur dneui; the damage had been staggering. It took nearly all of his underlings, plus those still alive on the destroyer, to get the ship ready to tow.

With the Privateer finally heading for home, Linda had time to reflect on everything that had occurred. Her hands started to shake and she felt the need to cry. She quickly rose and said, "Bill, you have the con," as she rapidly left the bridge.

Back in her quarters, Linda sat at her desk and began to cry. Her entire body shook from the letdown of being keyed up for so long. The entire adventure had taxed her beyond her limits. She knew that she would never live down the number of beings she had killed this day. "This is not what I had signed up for. I am not a cold blooded killer," she cried.

It took a long time for Linda to cry out her frustration, along with the shame she felt. When she felt she had full control of her emotions again, she rose and looked at herself in the mirror. She had purple circles under her eyes from lack of sleep. Dark streaks ran down her cheeks, like black lava from a volcano. "You're a mess," she told herself.

A light knock on her door made Linda jump. She quickly splashed water on her face to wash away the tear streaks. Her eyes were read and puffy, but lack of sleep explained that away. Returning to her desk, she said, "Enter."

Linda was relieved to see Bill enter the compartment. Bill looked visibly shaken as well. He walked over and took a chair without waiting to be asked. Bill looked as tired and worn out as she felt. Neither said a word for a long time. Bill just lay back in the chair and looked up at the ceiling.

A question suddenly occurred to Linda, "Bill, who is minding the Bridge?"

"I called Rebecca up to take over. It is good experience for her," he answered

"We will never be able to get this out of our minds, will we?" Bill asked after another long silence.

"No, I'm afraid not. You and I have accounted for the deaths of perhaps hundreds. There is no way we can justify or forgive ourselves for that. I have to live with it, knowing that every action taking by the Privateer and her crew, and this includes yours, were at my direction. I ordered you to fire on those ships. I ordered you to use whatever force was necessary. There is no way for me to take all that back. In fact, I can't really think of how else this whole mess could have been avoided. But I will keep trying to find that magical answer that justifies everything. I wish I could give you some words of wisdom that will help you feel better, or at least justify it all. Unfortunately, Bill, I can't. You and I are in the same boat, we will be haunted for years to come, I am afraid," Linda answered. She was monotone and emotionless. She then added, "If only I had taken Sharon's advice and just left. Instead I went back to help that ship and paid the dear price for it."

Bill was quiet again for a long time reflecting on Linda's comment. "It doesn't help, you know. Knowing that we were in a no-win situation and only acted as best we could. In the military you justified the kills by knowing you were saving lives in the end. Here it was different. We killed, but to what end? Sure, we got ourselves out of there, but what did we really accomplish? All this bloodshed over one stinking probe."

"I don't know what to tell you, Bill. Sometimes you get thrown into situations that become hard to explain in the end. And when you try to explain it, it just confuses you more. You just have to go on and hope that someday it will all just fade into the past," Linda said, trying to reassure Bill. She then added, "When we are docked and you are finally released from your duties, come and see me. I want to talk with you some more. Will you do that for me?"

"Sure," Bill replied and then got up to leave. Just before he opened the door he added, "Sharon is dead. She passed away just before I came down here. I wanted to let you know in person."

Linda just stared at Bill's back as he leaned his head against the door. When Linda didn't respond, Bill opened the door and exited without looking back at her. "Just great, more blood on my hands," Linda said out loud. "Poor Sharon, you were the most innocent of all of us, and I got you killed." She slowly put her head in her hands and started to cry once more.

Twenty-three days after reentering warp, the Privateer popped out of light speed into the outer segment of the Rapitine shipping lanes. A standard pilot vessel and two military escorts met them shortly afterwards. Several shuttles arrived loaded with curious sightseers eager to get a first look at the now famous ship. Along the starboard side, they could see a strange buckling in the hull just aft of the turret. Nearly a third of the emitters were pushed into the hull. As the Privateer passed by, they could see jagged holes in the aft end of the ship. The starboard exhaust port was also severely scarred from energy hits. As the shuttles drifted up, they could see where the entire top of the ship from the turret to the aft section was stripped of color from the plasma venting. Even the turret itself had a burned out look, mostly around the inner section where the barrels just stuck out.

Bill had the rare treat of being allowed on the bridge during exit from warp. Rebecca was sitting in emergency control. Linda had felt that Bill deserved this treat and volunteered her to take his place. Bill was awed by the reception they were receiving. Normally, the coming and going of ships was not shared information. He was guessing that the company had put their story out on the news wire for publicity.

"They will regret this release when they find out that the exec was killed in this venture," Linda commented, in a low voice to Bill.

Twenty hours later, the thrill gone, the Privateer quietly slipped into a birth within the space dock. She would be unloaded before being sent to the shipyard for repairs. The pilot ship signaled its release and went back to its berth while the two escort ships returned to the military docking facility. The first object to be taken off the ship was the crate carrying Sharon's body. The company was taking possession of it, along with the duty of notifying next of kin.

It took nearly four days for Linda and Bill to complete the debriefing before being called before the maritime board of inquiry. They both received their summons on the same day. Bill was slated to go first and Linda was to follow. They both sat outside the chamber door waiting to be called in. Neither said anything as they collected their thoughts. Linda looked over at Bill and gave him a reassuring smile. Bill stood up when his name was called. He entered the chamber with confidence, but nervous none the less.

"Please be seated," a grey haired man in his late sixties said. Bill looked at each of the five board members before taking the seat situated directly in front of them. Each of the board members were sitting at a long flat table. Their arms politely resting on top of it. Three of the members were men, the other two women. All were in their later years.

"State your name, rank and current assignment for the records, please," a clerk requested. The clerk was standing off to his left. In front of the clerk was a small table with a recording device. It collected the sounds from microphones on the table in front of Bill.

"Bill Launtra, Commander, Weapons and Security Officer aboard the Privateer," Bill responded.

The Clerk went on to note the date, time and reason for the inquiry. It was also noted that the inquiry had been called for by the maritime board. The clerk then ended with a calling of the names of each of the board members. Admirals all, retired.

"Commander Launtra, this board had been convened to determine if the officers acted appropriately aboard the Privateer for the events that were noted in the inquiry summary statement. It is the purpose of this board to determine if either you or Captain Eccles were negligent in the handling of the affairs aboard the Privateer, in accordance with the laws of the maritime board. Before we begin, do you have an opening statement you would like to make?" The grey haired man, Bill now knew as Admiral Saldana, asked.

"No sir," Bill responded.

"Let's begin then. Commander, when you were first ordered to open fire on the alien vessel, what was your understanding of the intent of that order?"

"Captain Eccles instructions to me were very clear. She wanted to drive off the ship that had already fired on us," Bill answered. He kept reminding himself to keep his answers direct and to the point. Don't volunteer information that may be misinterpreted, but also answer directly and honestly. Don't be vague, he reminded himself. It will only make it appear you are hiding something.

"Did you ever question why you would not fire a warning shot first," this asked by one of the other members. The admiral sitting on Bill's far right.

"No mam, the captain and exec were both on the bridge. It would not have been appropriate for me to question the orders coming from the bridge. I would have expected that the exec would have questioned the order if she deemed it appropriate to do so," Bill answered again. He regretted having said it, as soon as it left his mouth.

"Do you know if the executive officer questioned the order, Commander?"

"No mam, I was not privy to any of the conversations occurring on the bridge," Bill responded. He didn't like where this was going.

"So Commander, do you think it was appropriate to fire on the ship without giving them a warning first? Perhaps by firing a shot across their path?" This was asked by the admiral sitting second to the left.

"I don't think it is my place to say, Admiral, sir," Bill answered. Keep calm, he reminded himself.

"Oh, come on Commander! You are a high level officer and should have the ability to know what is appropriate action to take. So answer the question, should the captain have fired a warning first?" asked Admiral Saldana again.

Bill hesitated. He thought back to that moment in time and tried to decide if he would have done anything different. After a moment's pause he replied, "It is possible that a warning shot may have made some difference. But I remind the Admirals that we did nothing at this point to appear hostile to that ship. We were heading out of the system and we gave them no indication of any other intentions. This ship fired on the Privateer with the intent to harm. There is no question in my mind about that. When they took it to that level, a warning shot may have been interpreted as a poorly fired return shot. There is really no way we could have known or anticipated the thoughts or actions of these beings."

"When you did fire on the ship, why did you use three shots instead of one?" another of the admirals asked.

"The Captain ordered me to, 'drive them off'. I did not feel that a single shot from the plasma cannons would do that. Without knowing the makeup of the ship or what defenses it had, three shots seemed appropriate," Bill replied.

"Now Commander, turning to the events leading up to the Privateers departure. What was the rational of the intense firepower that destroyed the one alien vessel?" this from Admiral Saldana again.

"I take full responsibility for the destruction of that ship. When I fired on the first alien ship, the three bolts didn't disable it for very long. I wanted to add one extra shot in the hope of putting that ship out of action longer. It wasn't until I was able to see the impact that decision had that I reduced the number of shots. There was no way for me to know, prior to shooting, that the ship couldn't take the punishment."

As each admiral would ask a question, Bill tried his best to answer them. This went on for nearly an hour. Bill was mentally drained at the end.

"Commander, I have one last question for you. Do you believe that the death of Commander Sharon Bresee was negligent?" Admiral Saldana asked.

Bill was stunned for a second. How in the world could Sharon's death had been negligent? Bill looked down at his hands resting on his thighs. He moved his hands up and down his legs as he thought. He wasn't prepared for that question. It also made him cautious as to what would even make them asked that. Was that what this entire ordeal was about? For some way to push the blame for the death away from the company execs? What a bunch of horseshit this was turning out to be. He composed his thoughts again. He finally responded, "Sharon's death was clearly an accident. There was no way for the captain to have known that the Privateer would still be in danger when she asked Sharon to see to feeding the crew. Was it negligence? I fail to see how?"

"Thank you, Commander. This board will provide a written response to you of our findings." Admiral Saldana said, as a dismissal.

Bill turned and walked out of the chamber. Linda was still sitting there patiently waiting her turn. She looked at Bill and smiled that reassuring smile. Bill just shook his head at her and sat down to wait her return.

Sitting in the same hot seat as Bill, Linda waited for the clerk to read through the formalities. She looked at each of the admirals in turn. She knew this day would come. A death had occurred aboard her ship and she needed to be held accountable for it. Sadly, she thought of Sharon and how she had treated her. She only hoped that Sharon had taken it all in stride. Chalking it up to a finicky captain, she hoped. When the clerk finished his ramblings and she had stated her name, she returned her attention to the inquisition, as she saw it.

"Captain, when you found that the probe had been destroyed, why didn't you report back and receive further instructions? Instead of taking it upon yourself to investigate the foreign object further in the system?"

"I have asked myself that same question over and over Admiral. At the time, I thought it might have provided clues into what had happened to the probe. At the time, there did not appear to be any danger. I thought that having a better idea of what happened to the probe would be helpful," Linda answered directly.

"How can you say there was no danger? Didn't you just say the probe had been destroyed?"

"At that point in time our theory was that the probe had struck something and exploded. We did not have any supporting data to suggest foul play," Linda answered back with a little annoyance in her voice."

"That turned out to be a fatal decision, was it not, Captain?"

"Yes, it most definitely was. Knowing what I know now, I would not have proceeded further into the system. At that point in time, there was no reason to suspect danger. It was more of curiosity that drove me to go check out that monitoring device. Not a day has gone by that I have not regretted that decision. It would be easy for me to blame it on the company, or perhaps on being put into a situation I was not prepared for. But the reality is that I was put into a situation no one anticipated and I did the best I could based on my experience as a captain."

"Do you take responsibility for the death of Commander Bresee?"

"Oh, course," Linda had anticipated this question every since she arrived to wait her questioning. She continued, "As the captain of the Privateer I have full responsibility for everything that happens aboard my ship. Each of you Admirals know that as well as I do. It was my decision to send Sharon off the bridge. It was my decision to let her go when there was still a possibility of action, with two ships still lined up against us. Sharon is dead. No matter what I do from here on out, there is nothing I can do to bring her back. I wish there were. I have to live with the knowledge of her death, that my actions put her into a position to be killed. There is no greater burden for anyone to have to carry than that alone."

"Captain, why did you fire on the first ship? It seems prudent that you would have warned them off with a warning shot first"

"Up to the point that the Privateer was fired upon, we showed no act of aggression of any kind. That ship fired on the Privateer with the intent to put us out of action. To this day I cannot tell you why. They did not want us to leave. I knew, and it proved to be right, that that ship was trying to trap us. They knew, and I suspected, that there were more ships on the way. I needed to do two things. First, was to get more distance between us and that ship. Secondly, was to keep moving at all costs. I ordered the firing on that ship to drive them away from us. To give me more room to maneuver and to let them know that we would defend ourselves if need be. Firing a warning shot would only have invited them to fire on us again, perhaps with more determination."

"Then why in the world did you return back to that ship when it was disabled? That was a very foolish thing to have done, and I believe the real reason we are all assembled here today."

Linda had anticipated this question also. She had thought this over every since they had entered warp those many days ago. Even now she was at a loss for the real reason she turned back. It had proved to be a costly decision, and most likely the one that would sink her career.

"Admirals, I am not sure I can tell you why I turned about. It was a gut reaction at the time and a decision I have regretted ever since. That one decision, made in a split second of time, is clearly the defining moment when everything came into play. I know that had I not turned back, the arriving ships would have been too far out of position to prevent my departure. Had I not turned back, I would not have suffered the damage to the starboard side emitters that allowed that flaw in the deflectors. But I can tell you this: life is precious to me and I am not one to take it lightly. It was my feelings towards these unknown creatures that defined my actions at that point in time. I regret the decision, but not the morality of it. That is all I have to say on this topic." Linda nearly broke into tears.

The admiral on the far right asked, "Captain, do you need a short recess to gather your composure?"

"No Admiral, but I do thank you for that. Please continue," Linda said, composing herself quickly.

The admiral sitting at the center of the table looked at the other admirals. They each shook their heads as he looked at them in turn. He looked at Linda for a few seconds before saying, "Captain, this board has a very difficult task ahead of us. We will need to dissect that moment in time, your decision to go back, and try to make sense of it all. With the exception of that one moment, I believe that the rest of your actions were not only appropriate, but outright damn courageous. Before we adjourn, would you like to make a closing statement?"

"Yes, thank you Admiral. By shear coincidence, I had the opportunity to make, perhaps, one of the most important discoveries of mankind. The name of Captain Linda Eccles and the ship Privateer will be forever tied into historical records as the first alien encounter. How this is recorded will be decided by you five, here, today. I have no doubt that what happened aboard the Privateer will be turned into a teaching session for every officer training program, clear into the foreseeable future. It will be broken down, dissected and played over and over. What it will lack for all those future officers is the anxiety of the unknown. Missing will be the feeling of loneliness of command and the desperation of misreading what the other side is thinking. These young minds will review this from the sterile environment of a class room, without the shear panic of knowing the wrong decision means possible destruction of ship and crew. This will go down as either an unfortunate encounter that went wrong, or the missteps of a captain facing something never before encountered by the human race. All I can offer to you, in the hope you will understand, is that I was on my own out there. I was trying to make decisions not only to preserve my ship and crew, but also to try and salvage a first encounter. I was successful in the first, but failed miserable in the latter. What another captain would have done in this exact same situation, we may never know. I would hope they would have fared better."

"Thank you for your time, Captain. This hearing is now closed. You will be notified in writing of our decision."

Linda nodded to each of the admirals, turned and left the room. Once outside, she caught up with Bill, still waiting patiently for her. "I know a great little bar about ten minutes walk from here. Interested," Linda asked.

Bill looked at Linda, smiled and said, "Sure, why not."

With the inquiries over, Linda returned aboard the Privateer to supervise the last of the details before her ship was pulled into the shipyards for repairs and refit. With that weight off her shoulders, she moved into her cabin aboard the station. With nothing left to occupy her mind, she often thought back on the Privateer's adventure in minute detail. Nightmares haunted her sleep, mostly of Sharon needing help and always being just inches beyond her reach.

    Bill stayed mostly in his cabin and tried to catch up on current events. He watched a lot of the news wires but always turned it whenever the Privateer was discussed. He thought long and hard about taking that trip to the planet surface and camping out. Being away from everything sounded like a good idea. He thought back to the conversation that Linda and Bill had, in the bar shortly after the board hearings. Linda said that she wanted to talk with him, but only when the time was right. She told Bill that when he was ready to talk, to come see her. Bill thought it over and decided that he was about as ready as he would ever be.

    Standing outside the door to the Linda's cabin, Bill was pulled between knocking or just giving it more time. The door opened while he was still trying to decide. "You planning on camping out here in the hallway, Bill?" Linda asked.

    "No, I was trying to decide if I was ready to talk or not," he responded, somberly.

    "Well, while you are deciding, would you like a cup of coffee?" Linda asked.

    "I think I would," he said as he entered. Linda moved aside to let him in.

    Once Bill was seated and had a cup of coffee in hand, he asked, "How did you know I was standing outside the door."

    "I just had a feeling someone was there. I looked through the peephole and there you were, looking confused like a little lost boy," Linda joked.

    "That about sums it up all right. I feel lost and confused, "Bill offered.

They both drank some of their coffee, neither saying anything. Linda finally broke the silence, "Bill, I owe you a huge apology. I did something I am not at all proud of. But I felt it needed to be done and I took advantage of the situation to make it happen." Bill gave Linda a look of curiosity. Linda continued when he didn't say anything. "Bill, I knew that Sharon, God rest her sole, was offloading her duties onto you while sitting in her cabin crying over her boyfriend's picture. I let her do it because I was selfish and wanted to take advantage of it. Truth be known, I wanted you to learn how to run the day-to-day operations of the Privateer, and I knew that Sharon would force that on you. You handled it well and this has given me the opportunity to offer up the exec position to you. You have deserved it and I hope that you will accept it. I know this was a rotten thing to do, but I feel it was done for the right reasons. So what do you say? You want to help me run the Privateer? This assumes, however, that I will not be found incompetent and released of command."

Bill smiled as he answered, "I had a sneaky suspicion that you knew all along what Sharon was all about. I never knew a captain that didn't have a good grasp on what was taking place on their ship. If the board doesn't pull my bridge license, it would be my pleasure to be your exec."

Linda offered Bill her hand. He accepted and shook it. "Welcome aboard Commander. It is a pleasure to have you serving as the executive officer aboard the Privateer. Now, I have one more duty to perform. I have here two letters from the Maritime Board, one for you and one for me. They were dropped off this morning. I thought it would be fitting to open them together. In these written words our future depends."

epilogue

Exactly twenty-one days after the Privateer had departed their predicament, two gunboats arrived. Nothing more than floating gun platforms with warp engines and shields, these ships could put a large amount of firepower into a concentrated area, in a short amount of time. Both gunboats arrived to the right of the minefield left by the bfnor torrnt. The closest mines exploded, rocking both ships, but did not cause any damage to the heavily shielded vessels. Following orders to clear a path, both gunboat captains began eliminating the remaining mines through accurate and deadly firepower. Both gunboats then moved farther in system. One stopped to guard the jump point while the other continued towards the nearest tracking buoy.

Eighteen minutes later, four fast attack destroyers arrived and moved inwards with orders to take up positions between the two gunboats. Nearly an hour after the destroyers arrived, three cruisers popped out of warp, followed by a large Defender Class battle cruiser. The combined firepower of these vessels was massive. The last vessel to arrive was the research ship Auspicious. The Auspicious began mapping the entire system, including each planet. Two cruisers took up station on each side of the research ship and the third shadowed behind. The battle cruiser took up station in the path where the Privateer had reported the arrival of the five ships that pursued them.

Once the Auspicious had completed its mapping and analysis, it set out on one last task. It took on board the tracking buoy that was now closely guarded by the gunboat. It was hoped that they could extract enough information from this buoy to learn the language and technology of the species that created it. The gunboats then took on the task of eliminating all the other objects, including the other two minefields, while the other ships started exiting the system. The gunboats soon entered warp, having left nothing behind.

From the data captured by the Auspicious, it was learned that one of the planets was prime for habitation. The Admiral on the battle cruiser thought that the planet would be a nice spot for a military outpost…supported by a fleet of ships of course.

The bfnor torrnt was put into the shipyard for repairs immediately after she arrived. The newly reopened shipyard was busy replacing four of the forward launch tubes with rocket launchers. The Council decided that all minelayers were to be armed as such, for added firepower. The Council asked for all minelayers to be recalled for refit. In the births on each side of the minelayer sat two destroyers also receiving repairs.

When the tracking buoys reported the arrival of multiple ships into the rhepp system, the Council knew that sending their own ships in would be pointless. They had learned that sending in inferior ships, with inexperienced crews, would just cost them more ships. They tried to learn all they could with the data relayed from the various buoys before they were destroyed. The order went out for the crewing of all their ships. Once the last of the minelayers returned, the Council was ordering a massive mining of space around their planet. They were determined to stop these ships from getting close to their home planet. They hoped that, between the large minefields and the remaining ships, they could discourage these beings from coming too close. The Council also sped up their initiative to move into the hillsides. They hoped to have the Council quartered within these protective hillsides, along with all supporting facilities, before any ships arrived around their planet.

Synska byf was rewarded for his valiant attempt to stop the alien ship. He was assigned as overlord of the destroyer njyfur lguunc and would take over command after it was repaired. The njyfur lguunc paid a high price for its charge at the alien ship. Nearly a third of the crew was lost, including the overlord and underlord. It was scheduled to be in the shipyard for an extended period of time due to the massive damage it sustained. All of the ships were being upgraded with shielding.

Due to the lack of experienced overlords to command ships, brk'erst was being given command of the bfnor torrnt. He was also elevated to the status of overlord, but would have to complete the testing once he reached the right level of maturity. He knew that it was a great honor to become an overlord without having to go through the trials. If he ever wanted a byf title, he would have to complete the overlord testing.

Because of the loss of the tuilmf and the large loss of krracts, jeftrk was stripped of his byf title. He was also removed from his position working for the Council. He knew that this meant he would never be able to earn back his title or status. He had returned to his ghugg to find that all but the eldest of his mating partners had left for more suitable males. He now stood before the lair opening looking up at the bright sky. He wondered if it really mattered now anyway. He had heard that a fleet of ships had returned to the rhepp system. He figured it was only a matter of time before they arrived to seek vengeance on those who had attacked their ship. Having faced them once, he had little doubt that they would be able to sweep aside whatever resistance the Council tried to put up. He wondered how much time any of them had anyway. He sighed and returned to his ghugg.

Overling v'sdntil received notice from the Council that a statement had been placed into his work record for him to be tested for an underlord title, when he reached the appropriate maturity level. For now, he retained his current overling position with the bfnor torrnt. He was already looking forward to learning how the new missile launchers worked.

Commander Sharon Bresee was laid to rest at her home outside of Wichita, Kansas. The ceremony took place almost five months after her death, having taken that long to return her to planet Earth. It was a private affair funded by the company and included military honors.

The crew of the Privateer received a Maritime Meritorious Action award for the ship's performance during the encounter. Each received bonus credits for their actions involving the attempt to recover the probe. The military also added in extra credits for the information they gathered and provided. All crew members were granted leave for four months, officers limited to three months.

The Privateer was expected to be out of service for about five months to repair the damage she sustained and to receive her scheduled overhaul. While in the shipyard, her propulsion engines were also being upgraded to provide more speed during sub-light travel. This was expected to be the last refit for the Privateer before her replacement in two years. The company was counting on the newfound fame of the Privateer to bring a handsome price when the time came to sell her off. This was bolstered by some current inquiries into when they were expecting to place the ship on the block.

The Mercantile Enterprise's executives made a change in the design of the new setup ships to include a turret style gun similar to the Privateer. The original design of these new ships did not include any weaponry because they could not justify the cost of the system, along with the crew needed to handle them. The experience of the Privateer's adventure changed this decision.

For Linda and Bill, they did review their board letters together. Bill's stated, '*Commander Bill Launtra, after review by the Maritime Board, your actions were deemed appropriate in carrying out the orders you received from your commanding officer. This board could find no fault in the action taking by you aboard the Privateer. It is the recommendation of this board that your employment with Mercantile Enterprises remain in effect and that you continue to retain your rank of Commander with the Maritime Board.*'

For Linda, hers stated, '*Captain Linda Eccles, after review by the Maritime Board, your actions while commanding the commercial ship Privateer, has been broken into three categories. 1) You did, by your own admission, fail to communicate back to the company representatives prior to taking further action upon discovery of the destroyed probe. 2) Upon entering a dangerous situation, in the taking of fire from a hostile vessel, not only failed to flee such danger, but did place the ship and crew in further harms way by such action. 3) Did, properly and with common sense, depart to a non-hostile location, to seek repairs and further instructions. While this board did find that your actions were questionable, it did also take into consideration the nature of the situation and the stress that situation would have placed on your command decisions. While the loss of Commander Sharon Bresee was unfortunate, this board can find no fault in your decision that led up to her death. You could not have known of the nature of the weapons used in the ships that fired on the Privateer, and ultimately led to the events that caused Commander Bresee's death. In regards to the actions taken on the alien vessels; this board can not fault you for your investigative nature, when considering the events that were unfolding. It is therefore the decision of this board that you retain your employment with Mercantile Enterprises and retain your command authority as captain with the Maritime Board. In addition, this board finds no reason to suspend your command authority aboard the Privateer.'*

Linda and Bill have not heard the last of the krracts. Neither have the krracts heard the last from those pesky humans. Both are slated to meet again in the foreseeable future. There is a storm cloud on the horizon and it will bring these two sides together once again. Look for the sequel to be out soon called, Krracts, The Return…

about the author

The Krracts Encounter is Bob's first attempt at adventure writing. The concept and writings for this book were produced over many hours of business travel. Writing has become a dedicated hobby for Bob and we can expect to see many more great stories. Bob is currently working on the sequel to The Krracts Encounter with two other books in the wings. Bob and his wife live in Bakersfield, California along with their three grown kids.